SAM HANNIGAN'S
WOOF WEEK

SAM HANNIGAN'S WOOF WEEK

WRITTEN AND ILLUSTRATED BY

ALAN NOLAN

THE O'BRIEN PRESS
DUBLIN

FOR MY **REAL** GREAT-GRANNY, **NANNY GIGG,** AND FOR GRANDMAS AND GRANDADS EVERYWHERE

First published 2017 by
The O'Brien Press Limited
12 Terenure Road East, Rathgar,
Dublin 6, D06 HD27, Ireland

Tel: +353 1 492 3333
Fax: +353 1 429 2777

Email: books@obrien.ie
Website: www.obrien.ie

ISBN: 978-1-84717-919-7

5 4 3 2 1
20 19 18 17

Editing: The O'Brien Press Limited

Printed and bound by Norhaven Paperback A/S, Denmark.

The paper used in this book is produced
using pulp from managed forests.

The O'Brien Press receives assistance from

Published in

DUBLIN
UNESCO
City of Literature

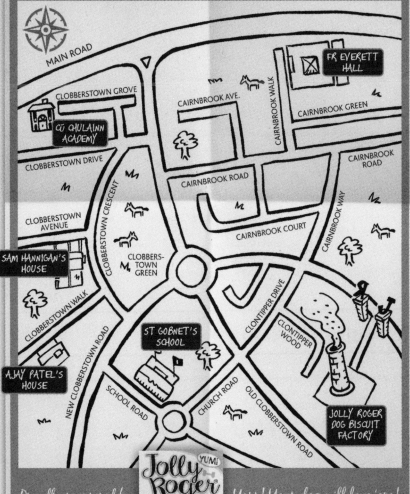

CHAPTER ONE
A DOG'S LIFE

Scritch. Scritch, scratch scritch.

Scritch again. Then another *scratch*.

And, after a while, just for good measure, a bit more *scritch*ing.

Despite having no intention of doing so, Sam Hannigan woke up.

What is that noise?

She lifted her head of shaggy, curly ginger hair off the pillow and listened.

She couldn't hear anything.

Maybe the noise that woke her up was part of a dream she was having? It had happened before – like that dream she had once where she was paddling her feet in a lake watching baby ducks splashing about beside a waterfall while her brother squirted her with a high-powered aqua-blaster water pistol and she really, really needed a wee and then she suddenly woke up and she was all–

HOOWWWWWWLLLLLLL!

Nope. Definitely not a dream. She had most categorically heard that noise.

HooWWwWWWwLLLllll!

She threw back the bed covers, adjusted her one-size-too-small pyjamas and padded barefoot across the threadbare carpet to the window.

She didn't bother to turn on the light – the bulb had gone a couple of weeks before and Nanny Gigg hadn't replaced it yet. Nanny Gigg claimed it was because she was afraid of heights and couldn't stand on a stool, but Sam knew it was because her granny couldn't afford to buy a new bulb. Sam and her brother, Bruno, had just started a new term in school, and schoolbooks aren't cheap.

Sam looked out the window from her dark bedroom. A huge yellow-ish moon hung silently in the sky like a big, uncooked pizza base. Mmm, pizza. Sam's tummy grumbled; she always fancied a snack when she woke up in the night. The trouble was, the fridge was usually empty. Bruno routinely ate any leftovers or treats that Nanny Gigg put back into the fridge after dinner. 'He's a growing lad,' Nanny Gigg would say. He's more like a bottomless pit, thought Sam. He practically inhales chicken legs, biscuits, bars, tomatoes, milk, orange juice and apple juice – he never leaves anything behind. Except for eggs, of course. The only food Sam's brother wouldn't eat was eggs – he wouldn't as much as look at an egg. Luckily, Sam liked omelettes.

Sam opened up the window and peered out into the long, messy garden at the back of their house. She could just about make out the rusty wheelbarrow that sat in the centre of the overgrown lawn and, beyond that, the silhouette of her grandad's inventing shed, locked up and mostly ignored since Daddy Mike went missing years before.

She listened. *Scritch. Scratch.*

Aaaah. She knew what it was – it was …

HOW-HOW-HoOooOoooOo ooWWwWWwLLLLLLL!

… next door's dog, Barker.

Sam craned her neck and squinted into the darkness to the left of her garden. Sure enough, she could just about make out a sandy-coloured shape moving slowly around in a tight circle in the murky night.

Ahh, thought Sam, *poor Barker. They've tied her up again in the garden. That's **so** mean.*

Barker was a big dog, a bit bigger than Sam herself, and Sam was a big fan of animals – big ones and small ones.

She loved all types of animals – horses, cows, sparrows, owls, moles, voles, crocodiles, koala bears. She loved dogs most of all, but Nanny Gigg said they didn't have enough money for a dog. For her birthday the year before, Sam had hoped for a dog but ended up with a goldfish. She called it Rover, even though the only place it 'roved' was round and round in circles in its bowl. She told all her friends it was a dogfish.

When her teacher, Ms Sniffles, asked the class to name the animal each child would like to be if they had a magic wish, most of them said they would be lions, so they could scare their brothers (Sam could relate to that); some said birds, so they could fly high over Clobberstown and away from school; but Sam said she'd just wish to be a dog.

'What kind of dog?' snuffled Ms Sniffles, blowing her nose on the sleeve of her manky jumper. 'A husky at the North Pole or a greyhound at the dog track?'

'Neither,' said Sam. 'Just an ordinary dog. A nice, old, tubby, friendly doggy dog.'

Ha! Be careful what you wish for!

How-How-HoOoOoOoooOo
ooWWwWWWwLLLLLLl!

Sam heard a window opening. Her eyes darted to the left and peered into the darkness. Something brown and shoe-shaped flew through it.

A shoe! thought Sam. *A size-eleven brogue, if I'm not mistaken!* (She was, it was a size ten.) Her thought – and Barker's howl – was cut short by the size-ten brogue connecting with the dog's rear end.

'Shut up, you dumb mutt!' roared a voice from the murk. 'Some of us are trying to sleep!'

Sam glared at the source of the voice (and, most likely, the shoe): Mr Soames – the Hannigans' next-door neighbour. Sam wrinkled her freckly nose. Mr Soames was always mistreating poor Barker.

Barker wouldn't be howling and scratching at the fence if Mr Soames didn't leave her tied up at nighttime, outside in the freezing cold. This kind of thing drove Sam bananas. She hated people being mean and cruel to animals. She balled up her fists and ground her teeth. Her face turned red. She stretched out of the window and yelled, 'Hey! You can't throw your manky shoe at Barker. She's just a poor defenceless dog!'

'Who's that? Samantha Hannigan?' came the voice from the darkness. 'You can shut up and all! Mind your own beeswax and go to bed, you interfering ginger busybody!'

Next door's window slammed shut, making Sam jump. In the darkness below she could hear Barker whimpering a sad, quiet, beaten-down whimper, her lesson learnt.

That bully, thought Sam. She stared out her window into the blackness for a while, then she nipped to the bathroom for a quick wee and got back into bed. Poor old Barker.

She was awoken (again) by a knock on her bedroom door. She sat up in bed and rubbed her eyes. Huh? Suddenly the boor burst open wide on his hinges, slamming into the wall, knocking a framed photo of an armadillo onto the carpet and making Sam's Irish dancing trophies jump in unison on their shelf.

Her brother, Bruno Brian Bartholomew Hannigan, stood in the doorway wearing his favourite pair of old, polka-dot pyjamas. 'It's your early morning call!' he trumpeted. And then he trumpeted from his opposite end.

PPAAAAAAArrRRrrR PPPPPPPPP-PPPPP!!

Sam jumped out of bed. This was a regular occurrence and she knew the drill. 'Get out, Bruno!' she cried, holding her duvet over her mouth and nose as she ran to open the window. The SMELL! It was atrocious! 'I can't breathe that, I'm a vegetarian!'

'Ahhhh,' said Bruno, showing his sharp, fang-like teeth as he took a deep sniff of the rotten pong, 'the sweet scent of last night's burgers, regurgitated just for you. Regurga-burgers, if you will!'

'I said GET OUT!' shouted Sam, She threw her alarm clock at Bruno, but missed and hit the wall beside the door where it smashed, cogs and little hands and bells going flying across the bedroom floor.

Ah well, thought Sam, *it didn't work properly anyway – a bit like Bruno.*

Bruno was eighteen months older than Sam and was almost a teenager. He was also eighteen centimeters taller, and much stronger. And quite a bit meaner.

He enjoyed playing dastardly, despicable tricks on Sam. Bruno delighted in being unpleasant to his little sister and was always thinking up schemes to make her life a misery. Most of the time this involved using some gadget or gizmo he unearthed in Daddy Mike's inventing shed. The shed was locked up and Bruno wasn't meant to go in there, but he considered himself to be a rebel (as well as a bit of a junior criminal genius) and had his own method of getting into the shed – wriggling in through a loose board in a rear wall. He regularly rummaged around the dusty piles of half-built inventions and crackpot contraptions that their grandad had been tinkering with before he disappeared. Bruno hadn't a clue what most of them did. He never looked at the notes or blueprints Daddy Mike had left behind, but that was the fun of it – trying out some weird-looking gadget on an unsuspecting Sam, just to see what would happen.

A couple of weeks before, on the morning of a big Irish dancing competition that Sam was competing in, he crept up behind her and stuck a dusty plastic hat-like device he had found under a pile of papers in the inventing shed on her head. The device was labeled Colour Change 2000, and it did just what it said on the label: when Bruno flicked the switch on the side it started to make a purring noise and in three seconds flat it had turned Sam's hair from a lovely gingery red to a bright fluorescent green! Sam, alarmed at having a plastic bowl with wires coming out of it jammed on her head, was even more alarmed when she looked in the mirror and saw that her hair looked like the main float in the Clobberstown St Patrick's Day parade. She had to wear one of Nanny Gigg's wigs while dancing in the competition. (Nanny Gigg had plenty of wigs, of all different styles and colours. She liked wigs almost as much as she liked hats.) The wig fell off during a particularly energetic jig in round two, and Martha Maguire and her sidekick, Abbie Cuffe – two girls in Sam's dance class – had slagged her unmercifully.

When she got back to the house, Bruno had another pleasant surprise for her. Under the pretence of giving her an apology hug, he smeared the back of Sam's coat with Stay-Put Putty, another of Daddy Mike's crazy inventions, and stuck her high up on the side wall of the house. Sam was stuck fast for an hour and a half (she had to admit it: Daddy Mike's inventions may be batty, but they sure *did* work) until she was spotted by her best friend, Ajay, who happened to be walking down Clobberstown Avenue. Ajay had to use a ladder to get her down.

But all that paled in comparison to what Bruno got up to on the previous Thursday afternoon. Sam came home from school as usual, and, knowing that Nanny Gigg would be out at her yoga class, let herself in using the door key she kept in her sock. As soon as she walked in the door, Bruno pounced on her from behind

and tripped her up by hooking his leg around her ankle. Sam ended up flat on her back on the kitchen lino, dazed and wondering what just happened. Her wondering was cut short by a shriek of 'Geronimo!' as Bruno leaped in the air and landed on Sam's chest, pinning her to the floor.

'Get off me, Bruno,!' she wailed. 'You're squishing me!'

Bruno took the opportunity to let go of a little fart – not a loud one like he did most mornings in Sam's bedroom, just a quick S.B.D. (Silent But Deadly).

'Holy moley, the SMELL!' Sam choked and gagged, trying to get her hands to her nose, but Bruno squeezed both her arms tight to her sides with his knees. She was well and truly stuck.

Bruno roared laughing for a few seconds, then he went quiet and his face became calm. 'Here, Sam,' he said pleasantly, 'do you like treats?'

Sam was so surprised by this change in tone that she had to think hard – *did* she like treats? 'Yeeeesssss …' she answered warily.

'But tell me this,' continued Bruno, 'do you like tasty treats?'

She again reluctantly replied in the affirmative.

'Do you like tasty, *chewy* treats?' Bruno was smiling down at her as she lay flat out – the sight of his mongoose-like teeth was a little unsettling.

'Yes, I like tasty, chewy treats, Bruno!' She wriggled, but it was no use; Bruno's weight was sticking her to the floor as surely as if he had coated her back with Stay-Put Putty again.

'But! Tell me this, oh sister of mine, do you like tasty, chewy, *crunchy* treats?'

'Yes, yes, yes, Bruno! Of course I do!' Sam cried.

'Okay, final question,' smirked Bruno. 'Do you, Sam Hannigan, like tasty, chewy, crunchy, *doggy* treats?'

'I said I do, Brun–' Sam cut herself short. 'Hold on, doggy treats?'

Bruno started to howl,
HoW-HoW-HoWWwwWLLLLLLL!

From under his jumper he produced a pack of Jolly Roger Dog Biscuits. 'I thought,' he said, giggling evilly, 'seeing as you like dogs so much, you'd probably like the same kind of treats that dogs do!'

With that, he grabbed Sam's nose in one hand and shook out the box of dog biscuits onto her chest with the other. Sam kept her mouth clamped shut and was struggling to breathe. Still holding her nose with one hand, Bruno lazily picked up a dog biscuit and gave it a sniff. 'Mmmmm. Meaty goodness …'

Sam had almost had enough. Her face, usually a pinky-orange thanks to her freckles, was turning an alarming shade of red. She gave in and opened her mouth to take a breath when, quick as a flash, Bruno jammed the dog biscuit straight into her open mouth! Sam's eyes gaped wide.

Bruno let go of her nose and clamped up her chin with both hands, forcing her mouth to close around the bite-size, cartoon bone shape of the Jolly Roger Dog Biscuit. 'Eat it. EAT IT!' he whooped.

'Ha haaah! I knew you were a dirty *dog*, Sam Hannigan! Good doggy! *Good* doggy! Ha haaah!'

He got up off Sam and, with a guffaw and a final tiny trumpet toot from his rear end, he stomped out of the kitchen, leaving Sam on the floor with a chestful of crumbs and a mouthful of dog biscuit. Sam let her head drop back onto the lino and tentatively chewed the biscuit. *It actually doesn't taste too bad*, she thought. *I wonder if there's meat in it? Ugh, Bruno – one day I'll get my own back for this …*

But today was Saturday and she still hadn't been able to think of a fitting payback for Bruno. She supposed she just wasn't evil enough to come up with a suitable scheme.

Sam stood at the bedroom window that she had opened to let out the smell of Bruno's latest wake-up trump and tried to think of revenge plan. Where did Bruno even get the dog biscuits that he made her eat? They didn't have a dog!

That reminds me, she thought, *poor Barker!* Like she had done during the night, she leaned out the window to look into next door's rubble-strewn garden. Daylight didn't do it many favours – it was quite a mess. Not as messy and overgrown as the Hannigans' garden, but messy all the same. She couldn't see Barker.

She clicked her tongue, *tlik, tlik, tlik tlik*, and called softly, 'Barker. Here, girl. Barker.' There was a creak and Barker stuck her head out from under a broken kitchen door that was leaning against an abandoned fridge halfway down the garden.

Poor mutt, thought Sam. *That's where she has to sleep. She must be freezing every night.* 'Good girl, Barker,' she whisper-called. 'Good, good doggy.'

Just then next door's back door opened and Mr Soames came out of his kitchen holding a sweeping brush and what looked like a can of dog food. Barker's head perked up and her pink tongue lolled out of her mouth.

Poor creature, thought Sam, watching unseen from above. *She's starving.*

Mr Soames stalked across the scruffy garden towards Barker, looking like every blade of grass his feet crushed on the short journey made him smile inside. His outside, however, wasn't smiling – it was sneering.

'Here, you dirty mutt,' he said to Barker, holding

up the can of dog food. 'I was going to give you this ' – Barker sat up, which wasn't easy for such a big dog, and started to drool. She really was hungry – 'but you were such a noisy, no-good nuisance pain-in-the-neck last night, I'm not going to give it to you.' He tossed the can over his shoulder and it CLANNNGED loudly against the door of a broken, rusty gas cooker lying in the long grass.

Mr Soames lifted the sweeping brush. 'You can have a taste of this instead!' With that, he started whacking poor Barker with the head of the brush.

Barker cowered and whimpered.

Sam was so shocked that she couldn't even shout out at Mr Soames. She ground her teeth and dug her toes into the carpet as she watched him walk back across his garden to the kitchen.

I'll get him for that, she thought. *One day, I'll get him for how he treats that poor dog.* If Sam had a naughty list (and she did), Mr Soames had just moved himself up into number-one position.

CHAPTER TWO
ANIMAL CRACKERS

'Mr Soames is such a bully,' said Sam as she went into the kitchen.
'He was being really mean to Barker. I saw him out my window.'
It was Saturday and she didn't need to be dressed yet, but after Bruno's
ear-piercing and pungent morning call and then watching the pitiful sight
of poor Barker being battered, she decided to get up, get dressed and get
out of the house. Besides that, Ajay was due to drop over.

Nanny Gigg turned around from the toaster. 'Old Soapy Soames is a
bit of a prune all right, in more ways than one – he's never out of that bath
of his. That's why he's always so wrinkly looking. And come to think of it,

I've never seen him wear anything
but pyjamas, even on the bus. He
IS nasty, though. He treats that
dog like doggy doo doo.'

The toaster popped suddenly
and, like lightning, Nanny Gigg
shot out her hand and caught the
two slices of toast in mid-air as
they soared towards the ceiling.
'Gotcha!'

Like the toaster, and, indeed, like the whole kitchen of 14 Clobberstown Avenue (or 'Clobberstown Lodge', as it proclaimed grandly on the wonky sign that hung on the gate), Nanny Gigg had seen better days.

She was skinny, pink and wrinkly, with mischievous grey eyes. Her hair, although frizzy and curly like Sam's, was steel grey instead of red. She always wore mis-matched, brightly coloured, baggy clothes and had a large collection of wigs and hats.

But what Sam loved about Nanny Gigg most of all was the fact that she was, not to put too fine a point on it, crazy. Not completely, 110%, paint-your-ankles-blue-and-marry-a-teapot crazy. Just a little bit.

Nanny Gigg was well known in Clobberstown for being a little bit loopy. She had been lightly loony from an early age. Before her husband Daddy Mike (Sam and Bruno's grandad) disappeared, back when Sam's father was a little boy, Nanny Gigg used to dress up in his school uniform and climb trees on the green across from Clobberstown Lodge, with all the neighbourhood kids cheering her on.

One day she got stuck at the very top of the highest chestnut tree and the fire brigade had to be called to rescue her. The fireman was very surprised to find at the top of the ladder that the little schoolboy he thought he was rescuing was actually a middle-aged lady in shorts, grey socks and a cloth school cap.

Another time, when Sam was a tiny baby, Nanny Gigg left her at home with her friend Marjorie and 'borrowed' next door's new puppy, Barker. (Mr Soames had no idea that Barker had been 'borrowed'.) She dressed the dog up in Sam's baby clothes, put a bonnet on her head, stuck her in a buggy and proudly paraded around the local shopping centre, stopping old ladies to ask them if they liked her 'hairy baby'.

Barker, being a nice puppy, was quite happy with all the attention, but the shopping centre security guards definitely weren't – they barred Nanny Gigg and her 'hairy baby' for two weeks.

But that was a long time ago, before Sam and Bruno's parents went to South America for their long, extended trip to catalogue the tree frogs of the Amazon Basin. Barker wasn't a pup any more and Sam certainly wasn't a baby any more, but Nanny Gigg was still a couple of custard creams short of a fruitcake.

Nanny Gigg placed the recently caught slices of toast on a side plate, adjusted her false teeth and hollered up the stairs, 'BRUNO! Your breakfast is ready!'

She turned to Sam. 'Sit down, luvvy. I've made you your favourite – pancakes.'

'Yum!' said Sam, delightedly.

'With tomato ketchup,' said Nanny Gigg.

Yak, thought Sam, despondently.

Sam shouldn't have been surprised. Nanny Gigg was a good cook, but she tended to do the same thing with food as she did with her clothes – she put things together that didn't really match. In the same way she didn't mind being seen in public wearing a lime-green woolly coat, with a purple belt around her waist and orange rubber clogs on her feet, she equally had no problem serving up a helping of Irish stew for dinner with a side order of fried marshmallows and a little bowl of yoghurt-covered peanuts. Sam had gotten used to the strange culinary combinations and never complained.

'Eat up now,' said Nanny Gigg. 'You'll need your strength for the Irish dancing tomorrow.'

Sam brightened up. 'Oh yeah,' she said. 'Nearly forgot!' She took a deep breath and tucked in to the tomato ketchup–covered pancakes. It was a weird combination of tastes, but it kind of worked.

'What time is Ajay coming over?' asked Nanny Gigg.

Ajay Patel was Sam's best friend. He was in her class at school and loved animals too, although the ones he liked best were more of the creepy crawly variety – in his bedroom he had a huge collection of stick insects, scorpions, newts and lizards. He even had a couple of snakes and a big, black, hairy tarantula spider called Tadhg. Most of his collection ate grasshoppers or crickets, but the snakes liked to eat dead mice. Ajay's dad got a pack of ten dead mice from the pet shop and kept them in the freezer. Once a week he'd defrost a couple of them and feed them to the snakes. It was pretty disgusting and, while Ajay loved his snakes (their

names were Stormbringer and Jeremy), he really didn't like to watch them while they were eating.

Ajay was a bit smaller than Sam, but he was a great footballer, and could do a trick where he would slurp a whole small carton of milk into his mouth and then swirl it round and round, building up the pressure until the milk squirted out his nose and then out of his eyes so he looked like he was crying milky tears. This made him very popular in class, although Ms Sniffles had to go home sick after she walked into the classroom at lunchtime and saw him doing his milky trick for a large crowd of schoolkids. This, needless to say, made him even more popular.

Sam got on with Ajay because he was loyal, a good listener (a handy thing, since she was a good talker) and because, whatever happened, he always stayed calm. No matter what the situation – forgotten homework, a missed bus or a last-minute dash to the pet shop for live grasshoppers – he never seemed to panic.

'He said he'd be here around eleven o'clock,' said Sam, polishing off the last of the pancakes.

'Grand,' said Nanny Gigg, looking at the kitchen clock, which was always fifteen minutes slow. 'I'm off upstairs for a bath. The next time you see me I'll be as wrinkly as Mr Soames' – she looked at Sam with one eyebrow raised – 'only much, MUCH better looking.' Nanny Gigg winked and trotted upstairs.

Sam took a long drink from her glass of cold milk and sat back in her chair. She loved Irish dancing – she was good at it and had loads of trophies. Ajay was coming around to play accordion while she practised. He played in the band of the same dance school that Sam went to, the Cú Chulainn Academy, so it made sense to practise together. Sam looked up at the fifteen-minute-slow clock too. Just ten o'clock, she reckoned. Ajay wouldn't be here for another hour.

A small scratching noise caught her attention, a tiny scritch scratch from the corner of the kitchen. On the floor below the kitchen counter, a little brown mouse was busily eating some crumbs that had fallen out of Nanny Gigg's cake sandwich the night before. Nanny Gigg loved sandwiches. She also loved cake. She hated to waste stale cake, so whenever there were slices of cake left over and going a bit hard, she'd stick them between two slices of buttered bread and munch away merrily.

Nanny Gigg's loose false teeth made sure that her gob was a world leader in the production of soggy cake crumbs, which made for some well-fed mice in Clobberstown Lodge.

Ahh, thought Sam, a little mousey! She slowly got off her seat with the idea of trying to stroke the mouse's fur, befriend it, house-train it, call it Molly and keep it as a pet, but just then she heard a much louder noise from the other side of the kitchen.

The back door slammed open. The mouse (bye, Molly …) scurried away in fright, cake crumbs forgotten. Sam jerked upright.

In the doorway stood Bruno holding a big, shiny red … well, Sam didn't quite know what it was. If she had to guess, she would have said it looked a bit like a vacuum cleaner, but with a sort of machine-gun handle at one end and a sort of trumpet spout at the other. The middle bit, though, was the weirdest part. In the centre of the cannon-like contraption, there was a glass goldfish bowl full of blue liquid. Floating in the liquid was what looked for all the world like a brain – it was pink and squidgy and had different coloured wires coming out of it and trailing up into the body of the gun. Above the goldfish bowl was stencilled the number '3000'.

'Do you like it?' smiled Bruno.

'What is it?' asked Sam. She deliberately answered with a question in the hope that Bruno would be confused and wouldn't notice her looking around for an escape route. She always got worried when Bruno smiled like that.

'This,' said Bruno grandly, 'is the Brain Swap 3000. I found it in Daddy Mike's inventing shed.' He held the device out from his body and gazed at it admiringly. It looked like he had made an effort to polish it.

'What,' said Sam, regretting the words even as they left her mouth, 'does it do?'

Bruno's smile faltered. 'Ah,' he said, 'that, I don't know …' His head dropped. Sam made a slight move sideways towards the door of the sitting room. Bruno's head shot up again. 'But there's only one way to find out!' he cried.

Sam turned and ran through the door, narrowly missing the side table that held Rover the goldfish's bowl as she dived behind Daddy Mike's old, unused armchair. She heard a couple of switches being flicked on and an electronic SQUUUEEEEEEEEEEEEEEE noise as Bruno came into the sitting room holding the Brain Swap 3000.

'100% power,' he said. 'The green light is on!' He hadn't bothered to read Daddy Mike's instruction manual, but any fool knows green lights mean we are good to go. 'Ladies and gentlemen, we are locked and loaded!' He didn't quite know what this meant, but he had heard it on a cop show and thought it sounded cool.

'Saa-aam,' he crooned, 'come out, come out wherever you are. I want to try out this baby on you …'

Sam furrowed her brow. Bruno was always being mean to her and treating her like a guinea pig with Daddy Mike's inventions, but not this time – she had had enough; it was time to make a stand. She got to her feet and came out from behind the big, tatty armchair. 'No, Bruno,' she said, a stern look on her freckly face. 'Put that thing away. There's no way you are going to use that on me!'

Bruno smiled a bit wider and pulled the trigger. There was a rush of wind in the sitting room, followed a schlorpy, schloorpy sound as a bright beam of blue light shot out of the trumpet end and hit Sam square in the chest. Sam's body suddenly went rigid. She straightened up, flat as a plank, the stern look still on her face, and then she slowly toppled forward, bouncing off Daddy Mike's armchair and landing on the moth-eaten carpet, her body stiff and her eyes staring. The blue liquid in the Brain Swap 3000's bowl bubbled a little, making the pink brain inside shift around and appear to be alive.

'Uh-oh,' said Bruno. His smile had gone. He reached out his foot and gave Sam's body a little kick. It stayed stiff. *Hmmm.* He looked at the gun. The small digital readout at the top read 'Power: 85%, Contents: 100%'. Bruno had absolutely no idea what that meant. Some people liked to do research before embarking on any endeavour, but Bruno fancied himself as a MAN OF ACTION, and MEN OF ACTION didn't do research, never read the manuals and were strangers to instruction books. *Who has time for reading*, he thought, *when there are trees to climb, sweets to eat, and sisters to torment? Not me!* He held up the gun and looked at the pinkish, doughy looking brain inside and wished he had read the manual for this particular invention. *Nanny Gigg is going to ground me for a month.* He gave Sam's rigid body another kick. *Wake up!*

He pointed the gun at Sam's body again as she lay on the carpet. *Maybe another blast will bring her back?* He pulled the trigger, but this time nothing happened. He tried it again, still nothing. He held the gun up and slapped it on the side, like he'd seen Nanny Gigg do with her laptop when it went on the fritz. The gun went off with the same rush of wind and *schlorpy-schloorpy* sound, but this time the beam of blue light sped across the sitting room, hitting Rover the goldfish's bowl and spinning it around, causing water to splash over the sides of the glass and soak the lace doily beneath it.

Bruno stared, horrified, at the gun and put it down on Daddy Mike's chair. The readout on the top said 'Power: 70%, Contents: 0%'. He backed away from the strange red device, wishing he'd never set eyes on it. *Of all the freaky gizmos in Grandad's shed, why did I have to pick this one?* His foot caught on Sam's stiff arm as he walked backwards and he fell heavily on the carpet, his backside raising a small cloud of dust.

'Help!' a tiny, squeaky voice cried. Bruno looked up from the floor. *What was that?* 'Help!' cried the voice again. There was a small splashing noise and a *blurbling* sound of bubbles in water. Bruno looked around. The goldfish bowl on the side table was rocking. 'Help me!' cried the small voice again. *Was it– ? That voice couldn't be coming from the bowl, could it?*

Bruno got up and walked slowly to Rover's bowl. 'Bruno! Help me! I can't swim!' Bruno's eyes goggled. In the bowl, splashing around in the water, was Rover the goldfish. Except it *wasn't* Rover the goldfish. Rover the goldfish's face looked almost … human. Rover's eyes looked up at Bruno and its lips moved as it opened and closed its goldfish mouth.

Bruno stared at the fish. He'd never really looked so closely at Rover before, but he would have sworn he could see freckles on the sides of its little fishy face.

'Bruno!' cried the goldfish. 'It's ME, SAM! Get me out of here now, I can't swim!'

'But, but,' stammered Bruno, 'but you're a fish. Fishes can swim.'

'Not this one,' said Sam as she manically flapped Rover's fins, trying to keep her fishy head above the water. 'I never learned! Our class was meant to, but the swimming pool was closed for renovations!'

'But you are a fish,' said Bruno. 'If I take you out of the water, you'll die.' Sam couldn't argue with his logic.

'It must have been the Brain Swap 3000!' shouted Bruno. He looked at Sam's stiff body, lying like a discarded plastic mannequin on the floor. 'It *schlorped* your brain out of your head and into the gun, then when I fired it again it must have *schloooped* your mind into the goldfish! This is AMAZING!' He did a little dance.

'Be amazed on your own time,' squeaked Sam. 'I can barely doggy-paddle here! Get me out of this goldfish and put me back in my own body! NOW!!'

'Oh yeah, right,' said Bruno, and he picked up the gun. He took aim at the fish and fired. The same rush of wind, the same *schlorpy-schloorpy*, the same blue beam. Bruno looked into the bowl. The fish was Rover again, swimming around under the water, freckle-less and as happy as any fish can be, unaware that anything unbelievably freaky and weird had ever happened.

Bruno looked at the gun. The pink brain seemed to throb in its glass bowl, its wires waving in the blue liquid. The readout on the top said 'Power: 55%, Contents: 100%'. *100%*, thought Bruno. *That must mean Sam's brain is locked and loaded in the gun!*

He looked around the sitting room. *Hmmm. No need to put Sam back into her body straight away. Time to have some fun!*

Bruno's eyes settled on a small brown shape peeking out from behind a curtain. *Aha! A mouse!* He took careful aim with the Brain Swap 3000 and pulled the trigger. The room lit up with the blue beam and the sudden wind blew back Bruno's curly hair. The tiny mouse was knocked up against the skirting board by the beam. Bruno threw the gun down on the chair and scrambled over to the curtains. He got down on his hands and knees in time to see the mouse pick itself up and stand up straight on his hind legs, brushing dust off its fur. It put its front feet on its hips and glared up at Bruno. 'Bruno, you rat – you've turned me into a mouse!' shouted Sam from the mousey body she was now inhabiting.

Just then there was a familiar mewling sound and Chairman Miaow, the white-furred Persian cat that lived on Clobberstown Avenue, came through the open window and jumped down onto the carpet, landing between Bruno and the small, mousey figure of his little sister Sam. 'Oh, hi, Chairman Miaow,' said Sam. Chairman Miaow looked at Sam and licked her lips. It was at that moment that Sam realised that she was now a mouse. Further to this, she realised that Chairman Miaow was a cat. A quite large, hungry-looking cat. 'Ah …' said Sam, and ran for it.

The cat chased Sam behind the curtains, up the leg and across the back of Daddy Mike's chair, onto the sideboard where Nanny Gigg's photo frames, vases and Irish dancing trophies from years gone by were kept, up onto the back of the sofa and back down onto the carpet. Bruno watched the chase with glee, throwing his head back laughing and slapping his leg with his hand.

'Bruno, you nitwit!' shouted Sam at the top of her mousey voice. 'Get the cat! Put Chairman Miaow out! Help! HELP!' She skidded to a halt, cornered up against the skirting board with no place to go. The cat slowly prowled towards her, growling.

'Oh, shut up, Chairman Miaow,' said Sam squeakily. 'You don't frighten me. I knew you when you were a kitten!' Sam drew back and punched the cat square in the nose with her mousey fist. Chairman Miaow looked stunned. *Miaow-huh?*

Bruno walked over to the corner, deftly caught the cat with one hand and dished her out of the window. He pulled the window closed so she couldn't get back in, and Chairman Miaow sat on the windowsill staring in and licking her lips hungrily.

Sam kicked Bruno in the shoe with her mouse foot. 'Bruno! Get me out of this mouse and put me back in my own body this instant!'

'I will in me–' started Bruno, but Sam ran up his trouser leg and bit him sharply on the knee.

'NOW, I said,' she squeaked from under the fabric.

'Okay, okay, get out of there,' said Bruno, rubbing his knee.

Sam came out and Bruno picked up the Brain Swap 3000 again. He aimed at Sam the mouse and fired the gun. He looked at the readout: 'Power: 35%, Contents: 100%'. *She's in*, he thought. *Now to get Sam's brain back in her body*. He aimed the gun at Sam's rigid body on the floor and pulled the trigger. The curtains moved with the rush of wind and Chairman Miaow, bored, jumped down of the windowsill and disappeared up Clobberstown Avenue.

Sam's body twitched and then stiffly sat up. 'You complete jerk, Bruno,' said Sam. 'Give that gun to me.'

She stood up and Bruno handed it over, inwardly relieved she was all right again. Sam looked at the gun – she didn't like it, with its nasty trumpet barrel and horrible pulsing brain. The readout on the top now said 'Power: 20%, Contents: 0%'. 'Yuk,' said Sam, handing the gun back to Bruno. 'Put that back out in the shed. And I don't want to see any more inventions. If you bring anything else out, I'm going to tell Nanny Gigg.'

Bruno, for once, did as he was told.

CHAPTER THREE
MY FURRY FRIEND

Ajay Patel sat at the Hannigans' kitchen table and listened to Sam venting about her brother. He had no trouble believing Sam's wild tale about her brain being transferred into the bodies of a goldfish and a mouse. He knew all about the shed in the garden that was full of Daddy Mike's wacky inventions – he had even been on the receiving end of some of them himself, courtesy of Bruno. One of them, labelled 'The Incredible Tan-U-Later', turned the skin of his face from its normal light brown to an alarming shade of electric pink. Ajay had to go to school with that pink face for a week, until the Tan-U-Later's effect wore off. Even the teachers started calling him Pinky Patel, much to Bruno's delight.

'C'mon, Ajay,' said Sam. 'It's a lovely day – let's practise in the back garden.'

Ajay hefted up his accordion and they trundled out the back door and onto the decking outside. They usually practised for Irish dance competitions out here when it wasn't raining, Ajay playing reels on his accordion and Sam dancing. Sam liked practising on the deck because it was old and bouncy, and she could get a good height to her leaps. Ajay liked it because the garden was big enough that he wasn't really disturbing anyone with his wheezy accordion music. Except, of course, for Mr Soames, and Ajay didn't mind disturbing that nasty crank at all. He smiled at Sam, 'Let's play it nice and loud this morning for Old Soapy!'

Soapy Soames! That reminded Sam of what had happened between Mr Soames and Barker the dog during the night, and she filled Ajay in. Ajay was outraged – he loved animals as much as Sam did and hated to see them mistreated. They walked to the fence and looked over at Barker. She whimpered a little and sadly raised her head in greeting. Her tail wagged weakly.

'That bully,' said Ajay. 'He shouldn't be treating poor Barker like that. Look at the poor thing, she's skinny and her fur's all stringy and she looks like she needs a good dinner. That rotten old Soapy Soames needs to be taught a lesson!'

Hmmmm, thought Sam, *a lesson* ... She backed away from the fence slowly, her eyes wide. 'Ajay,' she said, 'I think I may just have had a *magnificent* idea!' She told Ajay what she had in mind, and his eyes widened too.

A few minutes later, Ajay wriggled through the broken wall panel into Daddy Mike's inventing shed, and retrieved the Brain Swap 3000.

He brought it back to the sitting room, and then he and Sam had spent a while observing Rover the goldfish in his bowl on the side table. He looked fine, just swimming about as normal.

'See?' said Sam. 'It hasn't done Rover any harm.'

'Okay,' said Ajay, 'let me get this straight. You want me to fire this gun-thing at you, and then go out into the garden and fire it again, this time at Barker?'

'Yup!' said Sam brightly. 'How's your aim?'

'My aim is fine, I think,' said Ajay, holding up the gun and inspecting the horrible pink-ish brain-thingy inside. 'Are you sure you want to do this?'

'Quite sure,' said Sam. 'I've seen it work, it'll be fine!'

Ajay wasn't convinced. He read the small digital screen at the top of the gun: 'Power: 20%, Contents: 0%'. He looked at Sam. Her arms were crossed and she was sticking her bottom lip out – he knew from experience that she meant business.

'Okay, okay,' said Ajay. 'Stand over by the sofa. If you are going to fall, at least you'll fall onto something soft.'

'I won't be in here to feel it,' Sam said, tapping her head. 'Do it.'

Ajay took a deep breath and raised the Brain Swap 3000, aiming it at Sam's chest. 'Like this?' he asked; he still wasn't sure.

'I said, DO IT!' said Sam.

He did it.

The sudden rush of wind made the fringe of Ajay's jet-black hair stand straight up off his forehead. The *schlorpy-schloorpy* sound echoed around the room as the blue beam hit Sam again in the chest. Just like before, her body went completely stiff and straight, and then toppled over like a felled tree trunk onto the soft sofa cushions. 'Tim-berrr,' said Ajay quietly. He goggled at the Brain Swap 3000. The pink brain thingamabob pulsed and throbbed in its glass bowl. *Was Sam's brain in there?*

Okay, thought Ajay, *the next part of the plan*. He marched out into the garden, holding the gun carefully, afraid that Sam's brain might get hurt if he banged it off a wall or dropped it. He walked to the fence and peered into Mr Soames's garden. 'Barker!' he called. 'Here, girl!'

Barker obediently emerged from under the broken kitchen door and trotted warily over to Ajay, as close as the chain she was attached to would allow. 'Stay still now, good doggy,' said Ajay softly, and he levelled the gun at the dog. Barker sat on the other side of the fence, looking up at him mildly.

'I hope this works,' said Ajay to himself through gritted teeth as he pulled the trigger. The blue beam that came out of the trumpet end of the Brain Swap 3000 looked paler in the outdoor sunlight, and the rush of wind that seemed so strong indoors just felt like a light breeze, but the *schlorpy, schloorpy* sound was the same. Ajay didn't care for the sound – it sounded like the sound his dad made with a rubber-topped plunger when their loo was blocked. *Schlorpy, schloorpy*. Yuk.

Ajay looked down at Barker, who had toppled sideways onto the ground with the force of the blast. 'Sam?' he said, his voice all trembly. 'Sam, did it work? Is that ... YOU?'

Barker looked up at Ajay sadly. Then the dog's face seemed to break into a happy smile. She hopped up on her hind legs and started to dance a jig, the chain she was attached to jangling softly as she jumped. Sam's tongue lolled wildly out of her doggy mouth.

'It's ME!' cried Sam, her paws high in the air. 'It worked, Ajay! IT WORKED!'

'Oh. My. Giddy. Auntie. Ganita,' said Ajay.

Sam howled.

HoW-How-HowWwwWLLLLLLl!

'Okay,' she said. 'First things first – get me off this chain.' Her voice sounded a bit growlier than normal, but it was still definitely Sam's voice coming from the furry dog.

Ajay scrambled over the fence. He glanced up at Mr Soames' kitchen and then unhooked the chain from Barker's (or should that be Sam's?) collar.

Sam stretched her paws and arched her doggy back. Poor Barker, how did she put up with being chained like that?

Ajay looked like he was still slightly in shock. 'This is SO weird,' he said. He looked at Sam's face – it was still exactly like Barker's, but now it looked a bit like Sam's too. There even seemed to be freckles on her muzzle. 'How does it feel to be so … hairy?'

Sam let out a barky laugh and winked one of her new canine eyes at Ajay. 'Right,' she said, 'now it's time for phase two of the plan. Did you bring the tin opener?'

Ajay took it out of his pocket and held it up.

'Great,' said Sam. 'Mr Soames probably keeps the dog food in the kitchen. Let's go.'

They walked up Mr Soames's garden to the kitchen door, keeping an eye on the windows for movement. They didn't want to be caught before phase three of the plan kicked into action.

Ajay reached out his hand and tried the door. 'Locked,' he whispered, looking around at Sam.

'Dog flap!' whisper-growled Sam, and she pushed at the door's large dog flap with her hairy nose. It swung silently open. 'I'll go in and open up the door from the inside.' Sam squirmed her doggy body through the flap and into Mr Soames's kitchen.

It was empty. Sam stood up on her hind legs and tried to turn the door key with her paws. Although Barker's paws were a bit more mobile now Sam was in charge, they were still too clumsy to turn the key. *Hold on*, thought Sam, *if I can fit through the dog flap, so can Ajay!* She stuck her nose back though the flap. 'Hey, Ajay,' she whispered. 'Come in this way too!'

'Well, duh,' said Ajay, and crawled through. When he was in the kitchen he turned the key to unlock the door. 'In case we need to make a quick getaway.'

'Good thinking, Buffalo Bill,' replied Sam.

Isn't it weird, thought Ajay, *to be called Buffalo Bill by my best friend, who is now a dog?*

'Now,' said Sam the dog, opening up a kitchen press, 'let's get opening some dog food cans.'

While Ajay opened up the cans with the tin opener he had brought, Sam padded quietly around the house, looking for Mr Soames. She found him, as she expected, in the bath, lying in a mountain of bubbles with a towel wrapped around his head and cucumber slices on his eyes. He had lit candles and placed them all around the rim of the bath. Soft pan pipe music was playing and he didn't notice Sam's furry nose nosing in the door.

Sam padded back down the stairs to the kitchen. 'It's perfect,' she whispered. 'He's in the bath right now!'

Ajay had opened about ten cans of stinky, wet dog food and emptied them into a big plastic bowl he found in one of the cupboards.

'Ready?' asked Sam.

'Ready,' said Ajay.

They both crept upstairs and, outside the bathroom door, Sam stood as tall as she could on her back legs while Ajay placed the big bowl of smelly dog food into her front paws. *Hee, this is going to be fun!*

Sam burst into the bathroom in all her doggy glory, barking as she did so. Mr Soames sat up in his bath, causing a small tidal wave of soapy water which splashed over the side. The cucumber slices slid off his eyes and he saw the big, hairy dog standing upright in the doorway, holding what looked like his second-best plastic bowl.

'B-B-B-Barker?' he said, incredulous.

'Yes! It's *me*, Barker!' boomed Sam, in her deepest doggy growl. 'And I'm sick of the way you bully me, you – you old, bully!'

Mr Soames would have jumped out of his socks in fright, but as he was in the bath, he wasn't wearing any.

'B-b-b-but, B-B-Barker, I-I-I-I d-didn't mean to–'

'Apology not accepted!' roared Sam. 'You know what happens to big, mean old dog-hating tyrants who beat dogs and starve them? They get a taste of their own medicine!'

With that, Sam tipped the bowl of runny, chunky, meaty dog food all over Mr Soames. A high-pitched SQUEAAAALLLLLL started to come out of his mouth. Meaty chunks of dog food floated beside him in the bubbles and Mr Soames frantically tried to bat them away with his back scrubber.

'I want you to treat me properly in future – lots of food, lots of walks and lots of treats – and I want a nice, warm new kennel!' Sam bared her canine canines. 'You better start being nice to me, or you'll find out that my BITE is much worse than my BARK!'

Sam started barking loudly, making Mr Soames cringe back in his bubbles. She turned and walked on her hind legs out of the bathroom and slammed the door. Ajay was outside, his brown eyes wide open in amazement. 'That. Was. Brilliant!'

'C'mon, Ajay,' said Sam. 'Time to turn tail and run for it!'

Back at Clobberstown Lodge, Ajay sat giggling on the sitting room sofa while Sam walked around the room wagging her long tail excitedly. Now that was a weird feeling – the more Sam wagged her tail, the happier she got. So this is what it's like to be a dog, thought Sam. She went to look at her wrist watch but realised there was no watch there on Barker's furry front paw. Ajay checked his watch: 'Five past twelve.'

'Great,' said Sam. 'Nanny Gigg won't be home from her art class for another half hour at least.'

They stood up, shifted the sofa and dragged Sam's body out from behind it. They had hidden it there, covered by a tartan blanket, just in case Nanny Gigg or Bruno walked in and wondered why Sam was lying there, stiff as a log of wood.

'Right,' said Sam, brushing down her fur, 'let's get my brain back into my body.'

Ajay retrieved the Brain Swap 3000 from behind Daddy Mike's old armchair and flicked the ON switch. The gun make a pathetic SSQUEEEEEEE noise and then started beeping softly, BEEP BEEP BEEP BEEP.

'Problem?' asked Sam, scratching her floppy, hairy ear with her back paw.

Ajay looked at the readout. 'Power: 0%, Contents: 0%.' 'Uh-oh,' he said softly.

'Uh-oh?' said Sam. 'I don't like uh-oh. I never like an uh-oh.'

Ajay's face turned pale. 'Sam, I think the gun may be out of charge.'

'WHAT?!' Sam grabbed the gun in her furry paws.

'Check out at the readout on the top,' said Ajay. 'Power: 0%, Contents: 0%.'

Sam looked. That's what it said, all right. 'No problem. We'll just recharge it and try again later.' She picked up a small hand mirror that Nanny Gigg liked to use when she was trying on her hats and looked at her hairy, doggy face. She brushed a strand of fur out of her eyes with her paw. 'It's okay, I don't mind being Barker for a little while longer. As long as Nanny Gigg doesn't find out.'

Just then, there was the sound of a key turning in the front door. Sam and Ajay looked at each other in horror.

'Nanny Gigg?' said Ajay.

'She's back early from art class!' said Sam. 'Quick, Ajay – help me hide my body!'

They quickly flung Sam's human body back behind the sofa. Sam sat on Daddy Mike's chair and covered up most of her doggy body with the blanket. Ajay leaned up against the side of the armchair, trying to look casual, as Nanny Gigg walked into the sitting room.

'Ah, there you are, kids,' she said, taking off her hat (a bright green

Robin Hood-style one with a long brown feather) and placing it on the sideboard. 'Art class had to end early today. Lizzie Taite was trying to draw Spiderman and was making a bags of it and started to cry. I wouldn't mind, but Lizzie Taite is well into her seventies and should know better. The teacher had to bring her off for a pot of tea to calm her down. Are you finished with your Irish dancing?'

'Eh,' said Sam, pulling the tartan blanket up to her hairy chin with her paw, 'yes. Yeah, all done.'

'Well, the best of luck with the competition tomorrow,' said Nanny Gigg. 'You'll be brilliant, as always. You too, Ajay – you sure can make that accordion sing.'

She walked out of the sitting room, and Sam and Ajay listened as she went up the rickety stairs.

'She didn't even notice you're a dog,' said Ajay in wonder.

'Nanny Gigg is lovely,' said Sam, 'but she's a bit distracted at the best of times. Not to mention a bit, you know, cuckoo.'

Sam stood up, the blanket dropping to the floor. 'Okay, Ajay, we've got to get this gun charged up again so I can get back into my own body. There must be a plug or a power charger out in the inventing shed.'

'I'm on it,' said Ajay. 'You stay here and I'll have a look.'

Ajay wriggled in through the loose panel at the rear of Daddy Mike's inventing shed. The inside was fairly dark. There was one big window and dust motes floated around in the beam of sunlight that streamed through it. Ajay looked around the various tables and worktops. All of them were covered in papers, and each of the papers was covered in handwritten squiggles and hand-drawn graphs and diagrams. There were also hundreds of circuit boards, valves, cog wheels, buttons, loose levers and dials with wires hanging out of them. Up on shelves around the sides of the shed were strange-looking gadgets, gizmos and weird contraptions of every shape and size. Some had lights on their sides, some had multi-coloured switches, some had grips and handles, some had curious spouts or nozzles. All were covered in a thick coating of dust. Cobwebs hung from the ceiling and Ajay had to brush them out of his face as he walked through the dim shed to the shelf where he had found the Brain Swap 3000.

He reached up to the high shelf and felt around for a plug or charger, but there was none. His hand felt a paper folder, and he took it down and looked at the cover. In the shadowy light he could make out the words written on it in spidery handwriting: 'Brain Swap 3000 – Instructions for Use.' Well, thought Ajay, that may come in useful. He stepped back from the shelf and trod on a hard object. He bent down and picked it up. The plug! Bruno must have knocked it off the shelf when he took down the Brain Swap 3000 for the first time!

Ajay took the plug and the instruction manual and headed back to Sam. He connected the lead to the Brain Swap 3000 and plugged it into the wall socket. They both looked at the digital readout on the top of the gun: 'Power: 0%, Contents: 0%.'

'Oh well,' said Sam. 'It'll probably take a while to charge.' They both sat back on the sofa.

An hour later, the readout still read 'Power: 0%, Contents: 0%'.

Ajay looked through the instruction manual. Daddy Mike's writing was in a faded blue pen and was squiggly and hard to read. After a while he looked up. 'Uh-oh,' he said.

'Uh-oh? Not more uh-ohs, I told you I don't like them!'

Ajay looked pale again. 'Well, you definitely won't like this uh-oh. It says here that if the Brain Swap 3000 is completely out of power, which it is, it takes four full days – that's ninety-six hours – to charge up again.'

'Uh-oh,' said Sam.

'Uh-*huh*,' replied Ajay.

'So you're telling me I'm stuck being an ACTUAL DOG for four whole days?'

'Looks like it,' said Ajay.

'But what about school on Monday? What about homework – I can't hold a pencil with these paws!' Sam gasped. 'Holy moley! What about the Irish dancing competition tomorrow?'

The Irish dance competition! In all the excitement about exacting revenge on Mr Soames, Sam and Ajay had completely forgotten about it. It was the most important competition this year. Cú Chulainn Academy had been looking forward to it for months and Sam was their best dancer by far – they *couldn't* miss it.

Under Barker's fur, Sam's face went pale. Like it or not, she was going to be a dancing dog.

CHAPTER FOUR
DOGGED DETERMINATION

Sam woke up and licked her lips. She was so thirsty. She threw back her covers and sat sleepily up in her bed. She had been having a weird dream. Something about pirates. She couldn't quite remember.

She reached out to her beside table for her glass of water. *Hmm.* She must be sleepier than she thought – the glass was difficult to pick up. She put the glass to her mouth and, with half-closed eyes, drank deeply. Some of the water dribbled onto her pyjamas top. *Oooh, cold.* She opened her eyes and saw her reflection in the water glass.

Oh no.

Still a dog.

She had hoped against hope that she would have woken up and been Sam again, with her fur-free face and her ginger hair tied up in two ball-like buns, but here she was, sitting up in bed, covered in thick, shaggy dog hair. *Great,* she thought, *I'm stuck as Barker for four days ... and I bet she has fleas.*

After Ajay had gone home yesterday, Sam had spent most of the night hiding in her bedroom. She didn't want to have to explain herself to Nanny Gigg, and she didn't want to be laughed at by Bruno, so she shouted down the stairs that she didn't want any dinner, locked the door and, for the most part, stayed put.

She had tried to read, but her doggy paws found it hard to turn the pages. It was the same when she tried to brush her teeth – it took her fifteen minutes because she kept dropping the toothbrush, and she used up nearly half the tube of toothpaste because her new teeth were four times the size of her usual ones.

The only time she left the room was to creep downstairs to the sitting room to check that her human body hadn't been discovered and to check the readout on the Brain Swap 3000. By ten o'clock that night, it was still only up to 2% power.

Her mobile phone beeped and she took it out from under her pillow. It was Ajay.

Morning, doggy pal! the text message read. *Have you figured out what to do about the dance competition this morning? My dad is bringing us. There by 9.30.*

As it happened, Sam had figured out what to do about the dancing competition. She had practised dancing the night before after Ajay had gone home. She wanted to see if her new doggy body could do it, and, if anything, her legs were even springier now that they were dog legs. She was able to kick faster and bounce even higher than before.

She was going to the competition, and she had a plan to explain her dogginess. It would work. At least, she hoped it would work.

Sam got dressed as best she could, putting on her Irish dance dress and fixing the tiara in her hair. She got her socks on easily enough, pulling them up with her big canine teeth. Her shoes were trickier – there was no way she could lace them up with her paws. She'd have to get Ajay to do them in the back of the car.

Sam crept downstairs and peeked into the kitchen. Nanny Gigg was in there at the sink, her back turned to the doorway.

'Is that you, Sam?' Nanny Gigg asked, without turning. 'Are you hungry? I can put some more pancakes on for you, but I'm afraid we're all out of ketchup, love.'

'That's okay, Nanny Gigg,' said Sam. 'I don't fancy pancakes this morning.' Sam actually fancied something else. She started thinking about dog biscuits and her mouth began to water. She wondered if Bruno still had that packet of Jolly Rogers in his room, the one he had held her down and fed to her. *Hold on!* she thought, as a terrible notion came into her head. *I'm a vegetarian – I can't eat dog biscuits, I have no idea what goes into them!* She guessed that as well as the biscuit bit, there was probably meat in them too. They were, after all, made for meat-eating dogs, not for vegetable-eating humans. *Mmmmm*, she thought, unable to help herself, *meat ...*

She shook herself and readjusted her tiara. *I may look like a dog in an Irish dancing dress*, she said to herself, *but I am human!*

Nanny Gigg turned around from the sink. Her eyes widened. 'Ohh!' she said. 'Don't you look lovely in your Irish dancing gear!' She pulled off her rubber gloves and walked over to Sam. She picked some lint off Sam's dress. 'You know, I used to love the Irish dancing when I was a girl. I wasn't like you, though – I was terrible at it. Gruesome Gigg, the other girls used to call me because I was so rubbish at the dancing. At least I think it was because I was so rubbish at the dancing ...' Nanny Gigg trailed off, lost in her own thoughts of long ago. 'But you're going to do great today,' she said suddenly, giving Sam a hug. 'You'll make the rest of them girls look like bandy-legged eejits!'

She started to roar laughing (Nanny Gigg's laugh sounded a bit like the hee-haw of a donkey) and turned back to the washing-up in the sink. 'Break a leg, luvvy. I'll have something to eat ready for you and Ajay when you get back.'

Sam couldn't believe it. She knew her granny was bonkers, but Nanny Gigg *still* hadn't noticed that Sam was a dog! *She gave me a hug and everything*, thought Sam.

Just then the bell rang and Sam ran to open the door. She had a little trouble with her paws, but, to be honest, the door was difficult to get open at the best of times. The problem was, the whole of Clobberstown Lodge seemed to be leaning slightly to one side, which made for wonky walls, skew-ways skirting boards and dodgy doors. One Hallowe'en they couldn't manage to get the front door open at all and when trick-or-treaters came around in their costumes, they had to pass the sweets out of the sitting-room window.

With a bit of a push from Ajay on the other side, the door opened. Ajay looked Sam up and down, from the furry ears that perked up at either side of the tiara right down to the hairy legs that poked out from the skirt. 'We have a problem,' he said. 'Your tail! When you dance, it's going to wag around behind you.'

'I was thinking the same thing,' said Sam. 'I'll have to do my best to keep it under control. Just do me a favour: don't tell me any jokes. If I laugh, that'll make me happy, and if I'm happy, my tail will wag. I won't be able to help it!'

'No jokes. No problem,' said Ajay. 'Come on, Dad's waiting in the car.'

Sam randomly grabbed one of Nanny Gigg's hats from the rack beside the front door and jammed it on her head. It was a big red beret and it covered her hairy ears and most of her head. Ajay helped her put on one of Nanny Gigg's big beige raincoats and they walked down the garden path to Ajay's dad's car. Sam scampered in and Ajay helped her with the safety belt, shoved his accordion to the middle of the back seat and put a little plastic cage into the front. 'That's Tadhg in there,' said Ajay. 'He's a sick little tarantula – right off his grasshoppers – so Dad said he'd look after him today.'

Mr Patel let out a big sigh but didn't turn around. 'So, where are we going, Ajay?' he said. 'You know, you treat this car as if it were a taxi.'

'But it is a taxi, Dad,' said Ajay. 'And you're a taxi driver – that's your job.'

'This is true,' said Mr Patel. He looked in the rear-view mirror. 'Good morning, Samantha,' he said cheerily. 'I like your lovely red hat.'

Sam pulled the hat lower on her head. 'Thanks, Mr Patel,' she said. 'I like your, em, taxi.'

Sam liked Ajay's dad. He was a bit cranky but very good natured, and, like her and Ajay, he loved animals. His favourite animals were huge ones like elephants, hippos and rhinos, mainly because they reminded him of dinosaurs. He had a family season ticket for Dublin Zoo and he loved to bring Ajay and Sam with him – they'd run around from enclosure to enclosure, looking at all the animals, while he'd spend a whole hour staring at a hippo. Sam was very fond of Mr Patel, but she wasn't fond of being called Samantha. She liked the Sam bit, it was the antha bit she had a problem with.

'I ask again, where are we going today, children?' said Mr Patel.

'Father Everett Hall,' said Ajay.

'That is the other side of Cairnbrook, yes?' asked Mr Patel. Except he wasn't really asking. Ajay's dad had an encyclopaedic knowledge of the suburbs of Dublin – he was a walking satnav. He just wanted to make a point. 'That is a long way from here, Ajay,' he said. 'I will expect you to wash the car for me this afternoon.'

Ajay rolled his eyes. He washed the outside of the car and vacuumed the inside every weekend, whether or not his dad was on driving duty during the week. 'Yes, Dad,' he said, shaking his head

and looking at Sam, who giggle-barked.

'Oh, Samantha,' said Mr Patel, his eyes on the road. 'Have you a bit of a cough? Your voice sounds a little husky.' Sam supposed she was more of a sheepdog than a husky, but either way, she couldn't control herself – her giggle-bark turned into full-blown guffaws. 'You should get a cough bottle, my dear, it sounds quite barky.'

Sam kept Nanny Gigg's long coat on as she and Ajay entered the Father Everett Hall.

The girls from the Cú Chulainn Academy were already there, sitting in a couple of rows of plastic seats at the back of the hall. They were all in their Irish dancing finery – dresses with plaited skirts and Celtic patterns, their hair primped and curled – sipping from plastic bottles of water. Ms Clancy, their dance teacher, was very big on hydration and insisted they bring at least four bottles each to every competition. This was fine in theory, but in practice it meant that at any given time during the day at least two or three girls would be in the loo.

The loo in Father Everett Hall was right beside the entrance where Sam and Ajay were standing, unsure of how to approach the crowd of girls. Suddenly the toilet door swung open violently, clipping Ajay's elbow. Ajay didn't even have time to say OW before Martha Maguire stormed through, adjusting her tiara and clip-on curly hair extensions. Martha's eyes bounced off Ajay like rubber balls and landed on Sam's hairy, canine features. 'Holy Mother of Molly!' she exclaimed loudly. 'Sam Hannigan, you've let yourself go! I know it's you, I recognise the old, worn-out dress!'

She reached out for Sam's hairy dog whiskers and pulled at what she thought was a mask. 'OW! Gerrof!' hissed Sam. Of course the furry face didn't budge – it wasn't a mask, it was the real thing.

'Ms Clancy!' shouted Martha. 'Samantha Hannigan is wearing a mask.'

Sam let the coat drop to the floor. Her hairy arms stuck out of the shoulder holes and her furry dog legs came out from under the skirt. 'Ah janey, Ms Clancy,' said Martha. 'She's dressed up like a dog.'

Ms Clancy sprung out of her seat and the rest of the girls gathered around Sam. 'Samantha Hannigan,' said the teacher crossly, 'what are you playing at? Why are you dressed like that? We're dancing in ten minutes!' Sam gulped.

Ajay pushed through the crowd. 'Excuse me, Ms Clancy, if you will allow me to explain?' Ajay knew this was going to happen and had spent the night before coming up with a whole range of explanations, before hitting on one that he thought was the most plausible. He took a deep breath. 'Okay,' he said. 'You know the way Sam loves animals?'

Ms Clancy nodded, her face like thunder.

'Well,' Ajay continued, 'she has decided to dress up as a dog for four whole days to raise money for an animal charity. Called the, um ...' This was the bit that he hadn't quite had time to think through. 'Called ...' He was racking his brains.

'Dinners for Dogs!' shouted Sam.

'YES!' said Ajay, 'Doggie Dinners!'

'Yes,' said Sam, 'I am. And I'm taking donations, so if anyone has spare change please give it Ajay.'

'Hold on,' said Martha. 'Is this charity called Doggie Dinners or Dinners for Dogs?'

Ajay ignored her. 'And the best thing is, we are called the Cú Chulainn Academy. We are named after the most famous hound in Irish mythology. Dressing up as a dog for Irish dance competitions makes perfect sense!'

'Hmmm,' said Ms Clancy. The angry look was slowly sliding off her face like ice cream off a cone on a sunny day. 'Hold on a minute.' She strode over to where the judges sat and a whispered conversation ensued. A couple of minutes later she sauntered back. 'Right so,' she said to Sam, 'I've checked with the judges and there's no rule against dancing in a dog costume. As long as you've the regulation dress, socks and shoes, we're good to go.' She winked at Sam. 'In fact, they think it's a great idea, and so do I – the dog angle may give us just the edge we were looking for against the Clontipper girls.' She squinted her eyes towards the group of girls at the front of the hall. 'I never liked their teacher, Ms Ní Ghúna, anyway.'

Clontipper Academy had beaten Cú Chulainn in five out of the last six competitions, and while the two sets of girls were friendly enough – they mostly all went to Sam and Ajay's school, St Gobnet's – their dance teachers didn't like each other at all.

'Oh,' said Ms Clancy, 'by the way, Sam, the judges gave me some donation money for you. Remind me to give it to you at the end. And dig deep yourselves, girls. Dinners for Doggies sounds like a great cause!'

'Doggie Dinners,' said Sam.

'Heh, Meals for Mutts, more like,' said Martha, giving Sam a dirty look.

Ajay sat down beside Alfie Byrne, Cú Chulainn's fiddle player, as the Cú Chulainn girls *ooh-ed* and *ahh-ed* over Sam's 'costume'.

The competitions went on late into Sunday afternoon, with Cú Chulainn and Clontipper both outshining all the other competing teams, until they were neck and neck in the medals stakes. Sam performed even better than she usually did, despite being a dog – she took her usual spot, front and centre of the troupe, and her paws never missed a step and kept perfect time with Ajay and Alfie's music.

Martha Maguire, in her usual position directly behind Sam, stared suspiciously at the long, furry tail that stuck out of Sam's skirt and seemed to be wagging for joy as she danced. The crowd, which was mostly mums, dads, grannys, aunties and uncles, cheered hard for Sam every time she took the stage with the Cú Chulainn troupe and gave her cash after each competition for Doggie Dinners, which Ajay put into his accordion case for safekeeping.

The last dance of the day was the solo soft shoe slip jig, and Sam was up against Clontipper's best dancer, Rachel McGrath. Ajay and Alfie played 'Rocky Road to Dublin' while Sam danced her paws off, bouncing high and kicking in perfect time to the music. Although her rival danced brilliantly, the judges gave the higher points to Sam.

'Well done, Sam, you were awesome,' said Rachel. 'I LOVE the dog costume!' Sam smiled a big doggy smile. 'And that mask is just SO realistic!'

Ms Clancy was delighted. 'I knew that costume would give us an edge over Clontipper,' she said, throwing a dirty look at the other team's coach. 'C'mon girls, let's pack up.'

The dancers started to gather their things and stuff them into backpacks, eager to enjoy what was left of their Sunday afternoon. Ajay was packing away his accordion when Sam came over to him. 'I'm absolutely starvin', Marvin,' she said.

Ajay looked up. 'I think I have a sandwich in my accordion case, if you'd like it?'

'No thanks,' said Sam. 'I've brought my own food. Cover me!'

Sam looked around and, to Ajay's surprise, pulled a packet of Jolly Roger Dog Biscuits from her backpack, took one out with her hairy paw and started to chow down. Dog biscuit crumbs flew everywhere. 'Mmmm,' said Sam, licking her lips, 'these are delicious!'

'Are you SURE you should be eating those, Sam?' asked Ajay, looking at the packet. 'I think there may be meat in those biscuits, and you're a vegetarian.'

'But they're just SO yummy, Ajay,' said Sam. 'I can't help myself!' She reached into the box for another, but her paws, clumsier than her normal human hands, fumbled the box and it fell to the floor with a clatter in the emptying hall, sending dog biscuits sliding in all directions across the shiny wooden floor.

Martha Maguire bent down to see what had bashed against her dancing shoe. It was light brown and bone-shaped. She held it up to her nose and sniffed. A DOG biscuit? Martha narrowed her eyes and stared over at Ajay and Sam in her dog costume. There was something decidedly dodgy about all this ...

THE MIS-ADVENTURES OF MR WILSON & MS PIKE

NOW, LISTEN HERE, MR WILSON. THIS IS THE GLORIOUS CREATURE THAT WE HAVE BEEN TASKED WITH KIDNAPPING. OR CAT-NAPPING, IF YOU WILL. A-HAH. HAH.

OH, MS PIKE, THE CAT IS NOT THE ONLY GLORIOUS CREATURE ONE SEES BEFORE ME.

STUFF AND NONSENSE, MR WILSON, STUFF AND NONSENSE. PLEASE CONFINE YOUR REMARKS TO THE JOB AT HAND.

CAT, PERSIAN, WHITE, FLUFFY, ANSWERS TO THE NAME OF CHAIRMAN MIAOW. RESIDENT IN THE CLOBBERSTOWN AVENUE AREA.

DID THE MASTER MENTION WHY HE REQUIRES THIS PARTICULAR CAT?

OURS IS NOT TO WONDER WHY, MR WILSON, OURS IS BUT TO DO OR DIE

AS LONG AS I DIE IN YOUR ARMS, MS PIKE, I SHALL BE HAPPY.

OH, *DO* SHUT UP, MR WILSON.

TARGET ACQUIRED, MR WILSON. CHAIRMAN MIAOW SPOTTED BESIDE THE BUS STOP. A-HAH. SO AMUSING, IT ALMOST LOOKS LIKE HE'S WAITING FOR A BUS. A-HAH. HAH.

OH, YOU ARE SO FUNNY, MS PIKE. AND SO PRETTY. SO DEVASTATINGLY PRETTY.

OH, *DO* SHUT UP, MR WILSON.

CHAPTER FIVE
TOO DROOL
FOR SCHOOL

Sam woke up with a jolt. She raised her paws to her face. Still hairy. Still a dog. Ah well.

What time is it? she wondered, sleepily looking around the room for her alarm clock. *Oh, that's right, I threw it at Bruno and it got smashed. The day before yesterday. Saturday.*

The day before yesterday? But that meant that today was Monday! And that meant ... SCHOOL. Sam thought briefly about pretending to be sick, but she didn't like to lie to Nanny Gigg. As well as that, she figured, by this stage Martha Maguire will have spread the word all around Clobberstown – everyone at St Gobnet's National School will know that Sam Hannigan is a dog.

Or at least they will *think* that Sam Hannigan is dressed up as a dog for charity. She sat up in bed. *This is do-able. I can be a dog at school for a couple of days. No problem.* Sam stood up and looked at her furry face in the small bedroom mirror. *Holy moley. Let's get this over with.*

She had her shower, tried to put on her school uniform, gave up and put on her school tracksuit (which was easier as it had no buttons), and went downstairs to the kitchen. The tracksuit covered more of her body, anyway – you couldn't even see her hairy, doggy legs.

Bruno took one look at Sam and started to laugh uproariously, his body twisting into knots and kinks with glee. 'Shut up,' said Sam. 'This is kind of your fault.' She looked around the kitchen. 'Where's Nanny Gigg?'

'Sculpture class,' spat out Bruno, between giggles, laughs and chortles.

'Sculpture class?' said Sam. 'But that doesn't start until nine thirty.'

'It's five to nine now,' said Bruno, standing up and slinging his schoolbag on his back. 'Why are you so late getting up? Isn't your alarm clock working?' He left the kitchen on a mini tidal wave of his own giggles, titters and guffaws.

Five to nine? thought Sam. *No time for breakfast, I'm late!* She grabbed her schoolbag and trotted doggily after Bruno.

The whole way to school, Bruno tried to shoo Sam away – he didn't want to be seen walking with a dog. He even threw a couple of sticks into the road, shouting 'FETCH!' Although she was secretly quite tempted to run after the sticks, Sam was definitely not amused. She walked on her hind legs with her front paws crossed in front of her and growled in Bruno's direction. Bruno got the message and marched on ahead, still snickering softly to himself.

At the corner of School Road, Ajay was waiting for her, as usual. They always walked the last bit together, but this time he was looking hard at his watch. 'Cutting it fine, Sam,' he said, stating the obvious. 'We'd better hurry up or we'll be late!'

They were the last people in through the gates as Ogg, the huge but friendly school caretaker, was closing them. 'Good morning, children. Hurry along, the second bell has gone,' he said in his deep bass voice. 'Sam Hannigan, you look different. Have you done something to your hair?'

'It's a costume!' said Sam. 'I'm dressed up as a dog to collect money for charity!' She hated lying to Ogg. Everybody at St Gobnet's *loved* Ogg. He looked like a biker mixed with a yeti, with his long hair, huge monobrow, whiskery chin and massive, muscly arms, but he was the kindest, gentlest (and biggest) man any of the kids knew.

'Ahhh,' said Ogg, 'a dog costume. That'll be it.'

As Sam and Ajay walked off, Ogg sniffed the air with his mammoth-sized nose. *Hmm*, he thought. *If that's a dog costume, then my granny's a Neanderthal.*

Ms Sniffles was taking the roll as Sam and Ajay walked into the classroom. The whole class gasped when they saw Sam. Martha Maguire turned to Abbie Cuffe in the seat behind her. 'I *told* you, Abbie, didn't I?' Abbie nodded, dumb-stuck and staring at Sam.

'Sam Hannigan,' said Ms Sniffles in her squeaky voice, putting the roll down and grabbing a tissue from the box on her table. She blew her nose noisily and continued, '*Why* are you dressed like *that*?'

'It's a costume,' said Sam. 'I'm dressed up as a dog to collect money for charity.'

'Yes,' chipped in Ajay, 'Sam has to dress as a dog for four days to raise money for Doggie Dinners!'

'Dinners for Dogs,' said Sam. They really had to decide what this charity was called. They also had to decide what to do with all the money they had been given at the Irish dance competition. It was still all stuffed into Ajay's accordion case. They hadn't counted it, but it looked like a lot. 'It's a new charity that feeds abandoned dogs and gives them a home.' Sam would have loved if that were true. She loved dogs and hated to see them mistreated or hungry. As well as that, now she actually was a dog, she felt she knew what most dogs go through – she seemed to be hungry now the whole time herself!

'Well,' said Ms Sniffles, 'I think that is a lovely idea.' The teacher was a dog lover too, although she was a bit allergic – they always made her sneeze. She took a ten-euro note out of her purse and handed it (and a crumpled tissue, by mistake) to Sam. Sam gave it (and the dirty tissue) to Ajay, who pocketed the tenner and threw the tissue in the bin. Ew.

'How long is your sponsored dress-up going on for?' aked Ms Sniffles.

'Until Wednesday, fingers crossed,' said Sam. Fingers crossed was right. Hopefully the Brain Swap 3000 would be up and running by Wednesday – otherwise she might end up being a dog forever!

'Did you hear that, children?' said Ms Sniffles, coughing a little. 'If anybody wants to bring in money to sponsor Sam, you can do it tomorrow. Be generous now, it sounds like a great cause.'

Ajay and Sam smiled weakly at the class and took their seats. Sam's tail stuck out the back of her tracksuit and Martha pointed at it, whispering quietly to Abbie.

After little break, Ms Hennigan, the school's headmistress, came into the classroom. 'Sam Hannigan,' she said brightly, 'oh, you look magnificent! What a costume!'

Ms Hennigan sat down on the edge of Ms Sniffles's desk. 'Great news, Sam. Ms Sniffles was telling me all about Dinners for Dogs.'

'Doggie Dinners,' corrected Sam.

Ms Hennigan smiled broadly. 'Well, I have an old friend who works at the radio station – you know, Clobberstown FM – and she's arranged for you to go live on air to talk about your brilliant charity work!'

Sam went pale under her fur. 'On air? You mean, talk live on the radio?'

'Yes,' said Ms Hennigan, springing off the desk and checking her watch. 'Come down to my office where it's quieter. You're on in three minutes!'

Sam didn't have a choice; she and Ajay walked down the corridor with Ms Hennigan leading the way. 'We're so proud of you, Sam – what a brave thing to do, to dress up as a dog for four whole days!'

As soon as Sam sat down in the comfy chair reserved for the parents of troublesome children, Ms Hennigan thrust a phone into her paw. 'Here you go, Sam,' she whispered. 'You're on air! Be magnificent!' She took out her own smartphone and started filming.

Sam spoke into the phone. 'Hello?'

'HELLO! This is DJ Liz Anya on Clobberstown FM, broadcasting all over the Clobberstown, Clontipper and Cairnbrook areas, and I'm talking this morning with Sam Hannigan from Clobberstown, who is dressing up like a DOG *full-time* for four days to raise awareness and money for a charity that is very close to my heart, in fact it's one of my *all-time* favourites, Dinners for Dogs!'

'Doggie Dinners,' said Sam quietly.

'That's *right*,' said DJ Liz Anya, 'Now, Sam, tell us all about Dinners for Dogs and what you're doing to raise money.'

'Well,' said Sam, 'I'm dressing up as a dog full-time for four days to raise awareness and money for, em, Doggie Dinners.'

'Yeeeessss,' said DJ Liz Anya. Sam could tell she wanted her to keep going.

'Em, okay, Doggie Dinners, I mean Dinners for Dogs, is all about caring for stray dogs, taking them in, giving them a home, feeding them, and ... that kind of stuff.'

'Yeeeessss,' said DJ Liz Anya.

Sam kept going. 'The ultimate aim of Doggie, em, Dinners for Dogs, is to set up an animal sanctuary, not just for poor abandoned dogs but for all kinds of animals – cats, sheep, ponies, monkeys, zebras–'

'Spiders,' said Ajay.

'Yes!' continued Sam. 'Spiders, insects, worms, bugs, beetles.'

'So,' said DJ Liz Anya, 'you're *basically* rapping about everything from creepy crawlies to cuddly koalas?'

'Yes!' said Sam. 'That's a great tagline!'

Sam and Ajay smiled at each other. Well, Ajay smiled and Sam just stuck out her doggy tongue and wagged her tail.

'And *where* is this animal sanctuary going to *be*?' asked DJ Liz Anya.

'Right here in Clobberstown!' said Sam. She was getting a bit carried away with the idea – it sounded brilliant even though she was only making it up on the spot.

'That's F.A.B.' said DJ Liz Anya. 'Fantabulous And Brilliant. *How* can people give you money for this *wonderful* cause?'

'They can send it here to St Gobnet's National School,' said Sam, looking at Ms Hennigan, who nodded vigorously, all smiles, 'or they can send it to Clobberstown Lodge.'

'F.A.B.,' said DJ Liz Anya. 'Totes F.A.B. That was *Dog for Four Days* Sam Hannigan from St Gobnet's on behalf of Doggies for Dinner, a *fantabulous* cause. Next up we have local milkman and Clobberstown legend Patrick Mustard, who is going to talk to us about the importance of milk in our diets and give us all the goss about his *magnificent* moustache.'

The phone clicked off and started to beep – the call was over. Sam handed (or pawed) the receiver back to Ms Hennigan. 'Well done, Sam, you did St Gobnet's proud!' She reached into her desk and took out a twenty-euro note. 'Here you go,' she said, handing it to Ajay. 'We will have a collection in the staff room at big break as well. The animal sanctuary plan sounds fantabulous, sorry, fantastic!'

In the yard during big break, Sam and Ajay were surrounded by kids from all the classes, checking out Sam's 'dog costume', and Sam happily answered loads of questions about Doggie Dinners, or Dinners for Dogs, or Doggies for Dinner. *If there actually was a charity*, thought Sam, *it definitely would NOT be called Doggies for Dinner. Yuk!*

As they filed back into the classroom, Ms Sniffles called Sam and Ajay aside. 'Oh, Sam,' she said, shivering, for once, with excitement rather than her usual heavy cold, 'some great news: Ms Hennigan recorded your interview on her phone and uploaded it to the internet!' She held out her own smartphone, on the screen of which Sam could be seen, holding a phone to her floppy doggy ear with her furry doggy paw and talking all about Dinners for Dogs. 'It's got over two hundred thousand views already! And it's only been up for less than an hour!' Sam and Ajay exchanged glances. This was all moving *very* fast.

Just then the classroom intercom speaker BING-BONGed, and Ms Hennigan's voice crackled through. 'Pardon me, teachers and children, but could Sam Hannigan come to the principal's office immediately.'

What now? thought Sam, looking worriedly at Ajay. Martha Maguire snorted loudly in her seat, making Abbie Cuffe jump. Martha much preferred it when people were paying attention to her – she, for one, had had enough of Sam and her 'dog costume'.

Sam and Ajay walked down the corridor to Ms Hennigan's office and knocked on the door, which flew open before they had finished the first *tat* of *rat-a-tat-tat*.

'Sam Hannigan!' shouted Ms Hennigan. 'You will never guess who I have been on the phone to!' She was right, Sam never would have guessed. 'I just took a call from a researcher on *Bryan Hoolihan's Midweek Madness!*'

'The TV programme?' asked Ajay, his eyes boggling. 'My dad loves that show! And my mum loves Bryan Hoolihan!'

'Everybody loves Bryan Hoolihan,' said Ms Hennigan breathlessly, patting at her chest with a fluttery hand. 'He's such a dreamboat.'

Sam stuck out her doggy tongue. *Yuk*, she thought. *Adults ...*

'But never mind that now,' said Ms Hennigan. 'They want YOU to go on the show, tomorrow night!'

Sam couldn't believe her floppy, furry ears. 'Me? On the TV? Talking about Doggie Dinners?'

'Yes!' cried Ms Hennigan. 'This is a wonderful occasion! And a *fantabulous* opportunity for the school! I am so *proud* of you, Sam Hannigan! So PROUD!'

Sam and Ajay left the office, shell-shocked. First on the radio, then on the internet, and now on TV? There wasn't even a real charity called Dinners for Dogs. There wasn't even one called Doggie Dinners. If donations kept on coming in, maybe someone could start one ... *But holy moley*, she thought, *this is all moving SO fast.*

CHAPTER SIX
DIFFERENT DAY, SAME OLD DOG

Tuesday. Day three of dog-ness. Sam woke up and checked her face for fur, even though she fully expected to still be a dog. *Yup, still furry.* Barker's fur was so lovely and fluffy, but she preferred to pet it when it was actually on Barker – it was no fun petting her own face. She had a funny taste in her mouth, kind of rubbery and clothy. *Ew.*

The bedroom door burst open. Bruno stood in the doorway, holding up a newspaper and cackling with evil-sounding laughter. 'Did you see this morning's paper?' he managed to get out, between dastardly chuckles.

'Bruno, I just woke up. How would I know what's in the *Clobberstown Bugle*?' asked Sam, not unreasonably.

'I'll tell you what's in the *Clobberstown Bugle*,' said Bruno, smirking an evil smirk. 'YOU are!' He dissolved into kinks of laughter, the newspaper twisted and mangled between his fists.

'WHAT?' said Sam. 'Give it here!' She sprung from her bed and snatched the newspaper from Bruno's grasp.

It was true. On the front of the *Clobberstown Bugle* was a full-colour photo of a hugely hairy Sam, her ears perking up and her big doggy tongue lolling out of her toothy mouth. She was holding a phone. Ajay was beside her – his thumbs were up, but he had a decidedly fake-looking smile on his face. 'Oh. My. Dog,' said Sam. 'Ms Sniffles must have taken this when I was on the phone to the radio station yesterday!'

Clobberstown Bugle

EARLY EDITION

SIT UP AND BEG!

Local girl dresses as dog for charity

Local girl Sam Hannigan is causing *a stir with her fur* by dressing up as a dog for four days. Sam has pledged to be a permanent pooch until Wednesday of this week. This hair-raising stunt is in aid of new charity **Doggie Diners** and is already barking up the right trees, with interest from radio, on the internet and even a TV appearance on Bryan 'Call me Hooley' Hoolihan's Midweek Madness set for Tuesday night.

Sam and her comrade-in-canine-care and fellow animal admirer Ajay Patel have already collected a substantial sum in aid of Doggie Diners, and the aim is to open a sanctuary for stray, unwanted and unloved animals of all varieties, makes and breeds, right here in Clobberstown.

Continues page two.

Jolly Roger **YUM!**
Jolly Roger **YUM!** DOG BISCUITS

THEY'RE MIGHTY MEATY, MATEY!

ORIGINAL

Your Dog Will Love 'Em!

IN ALL GOOD SHOPS NOW

Sam read through the article quickly. It was all about Sam's efforts to raise money for what it called Doggie Diners, which was completely wrong and made it sound like a fast-food restaurant for dogs. At the end was a plea to send cash to the school or to Clobberstown Lodge.

'And that's not all!' chortled Bruno. 'You're all over social media – MyTube, Friendbook, Chirpybird, ClickChat, everywhere!'

He held out his smartphone. Sam groaned. She *was* everywhere.

'And by the way,' continued Bruno, smirking and holding up a pair of badly chewed tartan covered moccasins, 'Nanny Gigg wants to know what happened to her slippers.' Sam gulped. She had a vague memory of waking up hungry in the middle of the night, sleepwalking to the kitchen eating a sandwich while lying on the floor. She even had a memory of howling at the full moon on her way back upstairs. *Holy Moley*, she thought, *I must have eaten the slippers! Well, that explains the funny taste in my mouth.*

School that day was as hectic as the day before. All the kids in Sam's class brought in envelopes of cash for Doggie Dinners, and Ajay had to empty out his plastic lunchbox to collect the money. Martha and Abbie stood at the side of the classroom, looking at the spectacle with disdain.

At lunchtime Ogg the caretaker had to chase some camera-people and journalists away from the school gates – they were shouting out Sam's name but scarpered when they saw the massive figure of Ogg lumbering towards them. *Ha!* thought Sam. *They wouldn't run if they knew how gentle he really is!*

'Oh, Sam,' said Ogg, 'just to warn you: Ms Hennigan got me to make up some posters on the photocopier and hang them around the school.' He held up a poster for Sam to see.

SEE ST.GOBNET'S OWN
HERO HOUND!
SAM HANNIGAN
ON
BRYAN HOOLIHAN'S MIDWEEK MADNESS
TO-NITE AT 7.30PM

Sam face-pawed. *Brilliant.*

'That's great news, Ogg,' she said, slightly sarcastically. 'Now *everyone* will be watching.'

She and Ajay walked back to class. 'I'm worried, Ajay,' said Sam. 'What if I can't change back? What if I'm stuck being a dog forever?'

'Don't worry, Sam,' said Ajay, patting her head. 'The Brain Swap 3000 will be fully charged tomorrow – we just have to get tonight over and done with and you'll be yourself again in no time!'

But even Ajay looked a little worried and found it hard to concentrate on lessons for the rest of the day. *What if Sam couldn't be turned back?* He looked over to where she was sitting and, as he watched, Sam put her paw into her schoolbag and took out a Jolly Roger Dog Biscuit. She looked around and then ate it quickly and quietly while Ms Sniffles was correcting copies. Ajay wasn't the only one who noticed this; Martha Maguire spotted Sam eating the dog biscuit and, as she watched with a look that mingled suspicion with disgust, she wrote something down on a piece of paper and passed it to Abbie Cuffe. Abbie read the note, caught Martha's eye and nodded once.

Holy moley, thought Ajay, *Sam really likes those Jolly Rogers. And she keeps on scratching herself with her back paw when she thinks nobody's looking. AND I saw her drinking out of a puddle on the way into school this morning. Wait a minute – what if she's FORGETTING how to be Sam? Janey Crackers – what if she's actually turning into a REAL DOG?*

Ajay stared blankly at the class whiteboard. *The sooner the Brain Swap 3000 is up and running, he thought, and the sooner we restore Sam's brain to Sam's body, the better.*

THE MIS-ADVENTURES OF MR WILSON & MS PIKE

MR WILSON, WE'VE BEEN THROUGH THIS SEVEN TIMES ALREADY.

WE ENTER CLOBBERSTOWN FARM BY THE NORTH GATE UNDER COVER OF DARKNESS.

WE SWIFTLY AND SILENTLY CROSS THE FARMYARD, TAKING TROUBLE NOT TO WAKE THE ROOSTER.

WE QUIETLY OPEN THE BARN DOOR ...

... AND ACQUIRE THE OSTRICH!

CHAPTER SEVEN
A LOW DOWN, DIRTY DOG

Nanny Gigg's eyes goggled. She had never seen so much money. The postman had knocked on the door that morning with a sack full of envelopes, all addressed to either Doggie Dinners or Dinners for Dogs. Every single envelope had a fiver, a tenner or even a twenty-euro note in it. Some of them even had fifty-euro notes. Nanny Gigg took each note out, stacked it up in a pile on the worktop, and put the envelope in the recycling bin. Pretty soon the bin was full of envelopes, and there were four big piles of banknotes on the kitchen counter.

Nanny Gigg sat down on a kitchen chair, took out her false teeth and polished them with a dishcloth before popping them back in again. *Where did all this money come from?*

The back door opened and Sam and Ajay walked into the kitchen. Nanny Gigg looked up

from the table. 'Tell me this and tell me no more,' she said, pointing to the mounds of money on the countertop, 'what's the story-Rory with all this cash?'

'Ah,' said Ajay, 'well. You see. Sam and I have set up a charity, by mistake, and the cash is donations for the charity.'

'It's called Dinners for Dogs,' chipped in Sam, 'and the money is going to go toward feeding stray dogs and other poor animals.'

Nanny Gigg stared at Sam and squinted her eyes. She took off her glasses and rubbed them with the dishcloth. Then she took out her teeth and gave them a rub too. There was something different about Sam. Was it her big floppy ears? Could it be her furry face? 'Humph ong ah minnuh!' shouted Nanny Gigg. She put her false teeth back in and tried it again. 'Hold on a minute!' she shouted, much more successfully this time. 'Sam Hannigan, you are a DOG!'

'I'm sorry!' said Sam quickly. 'It wasn't my fault.' She blinked. 'Actually, now I think about it, it WAS my fault. I asked Ajay to brain-swap me with Barker with one of Daddy Mike's inventions …'

'The Brain Swap 3000,' said Ajay.

'… so I could play a trick on nasty old Mr Soames,' continued Sam. 'But the gun ran out of charge, and it takes four days to charge it, so I'm stuck being a dog until Wednesday.' Sam's doggy face crumpled and big tears started to roll down her furry cheeks. 'Oh, Nanny Gigg, I just want to be human again.'

Nanny Gigg opened her arms and hugged Sam's doggy body tight. 'Don't you worry one little bit,' she said. 'If there was one thing Daddy Mike was brilliant at, it was making things work. Before he disappeared he invented the Underwater Fire Extinguisher, Gloves for Chimpanzee's Feet, and he even developed a Hairbrush for Bald Gentlemen – and each of those marvellous gizmos had one thing in common.'

'They were all utterly useless?' asked Sam, wiping her nose on Nanny Gigg's cardigan.

'No!' cried Nanny Gigg. 'They all came with easy-to-read instructions and a six-month guarantee. But even more important than that, they all – every single one of his inventions – WORKED.' She smiled at Sam. 'If the instruction manual says the Drain Slop 2000 needs four days to recharge, then you can bet your bippy that at the end of the four days the Grain Flop 4000 will be charged up and ready to go!' She looked at her watch. 'Tomorrow is Wednesday, so you don't have to put up with being a dog for much longer. Just have an early night tonight and when you wake up, you'll be ready to get that brain of yours into your own body.'

'But I can't have an early night!' said Sam, her ears perking up. 'I nearly forgot, I'm going on the TV tonight. I'm due to be a guest on *Bryan Hoolihan's Midweek Madness!*'

'*Bryan Hoolihan's Midweek Madness?*' said Nanny Gigg. 'I LOVE *Bryan Hoolihan's Midweek Madness!*' That was no surprise; every older lady in Ireland was a huge fan of *Bryan Hoolihan's Midweek Madness*.

'C'mon Sam, let's get the glad rags on. We have to look our best for gorgeous Bryan Hoolihan!'

Nanny Gigg grabbed Sam by the paw and dragged her upstairs to get glammed up for the TV show, leaving Ajay in the kitchen. Ajay shrugged and started to count the cash that was stacked up in piles on the kitchen counter. As he flicked through the banknotes, he didn't notice two pairs of eyes watching him through the kitchen window.

Martha and Abbie watched Ajay count the money for a few minutes before creeping up the side passageway of Clobberstown Lodge and out the wonky front gate.

'I KNEW IT!' said Martha. 'Sam Hannigan IS a dog!'

'Ah, but it's not her fault, Martha,' said Abbie. 'You heard her. She didn't mean to get stuck like that, it was one of her grandad's inventions breaking down.'

'Doesn't matter,' said Martha. 'I KNEW she wasn't dressing up, I KNEW her costume was TOO real.' She smirked an evil smirk at Abbie. 'And tomorrow in school, we're going to let everyone know exactly what Sam Hannigan is: a no-good, cash-grabbing, Irish-dancing medal–stealing, low-down dirty DOG!'

CHAPTER EIGHT
HOIST THE JOLLY ROGER!

At the other side of Clobberstown, Roger Fitzmaurice, the owner of Jolly Roger™ Dog Biscuit Enterprises, the manufacturer of the world-famous Jolly Roger™ Dog Biscuit, and, he was proud to say, the face of 'Jolly Roger' on the front of the Jolly Roger Dog Biscuit™ packet, picked up his copy of the *Clobberstown Bugle* from the lacquered surface of his expensive rosewood desk and sat back in his comfy green-leather-and-mahogony executive office chair to read.

The headline on the front page of the newspaper immediately caught Mr Fitzmaurice's attention: 'SIT UP AND BEG! LOCAL GIRL DRESSES AS DOG FOR CHARITY.' He read though the article – some rubbish about a goonish girl who wanted to give free food to free-loading, mangy mutts – and then looked at the photo at the side of the article. He squinted his small brown eyes and looked harder. 'Goggins!' he shouted. 'Bring me my magnifying glass.'

Immediately a butler entered the large office though a secret door disguised as a bookcase, walked to the rosewood desk, picked up a golden-rimmed magnifying glass that was lying about forty centimetres away from where Roger Fitzmaurice was sitting, and placed it into his master's outstretched hand. 'About time,' said Mr Fitzmaurice without looking at his butler. 'Now get out, Goggins. I don't pay you to dilly-dally.'

'Yes, master,' said Goggins. 'Thank you, master.' Goggins exited the way he had come in, through the secret bookcase door.

Mr Fitzmaurice looked though the magnifying-glass lens at the photo of the girl dressed as a dog. Hmmm. Something didn't look right. Fitzmaurice knew animals – in fact, he collected them. That, in his opinion, was the one great thing about being a millionaire businessman and dog-biscuit magnate: he had enough money to collect anything he liked. And what he liked were animals. He had a large mansion in the foothills of the Dublin mountains, not too far from Clobberstown, and in the spacious grounds of that stately home he kept a variety of exotic and not-so-exotic beasts from all corners of the globe. But what he liked best were animals that were unusual. Animals that were one of a kind. He peered through the magnifying glass at the picture of Sam. A dog that could talk – a REAL talking dog – would certainly fall into that one of a kind category. He stared at the picture of the dog until all he could see were the dots printed on the newspaper. *If that's an idiot child dressed up as a dog*, he thought, *I'll eat my favourite wig.*

Mr Fitzmaurice stood up, walked to the enormous bay window of his first-floor office, and gazed down at the huge garden that was home to his private zoo. He listened to the growls and shrieks and calls of the diverse range of animals in their pens below, and then turned around to face the bookcase.

'GOGGINS!' he bellowed.

Goggins stuck his head around the secret door. 'Yes, master?'

'What took you so long?' said Mr Fitzmaurice, stroking his moustache. 'Summon Wilson and Pike immediately.'

'Here, sir,' said Mr Wilson and Ms Pike together as they stuck their heads around the secret door.

'You two blundering boneheads,' said Mr Fitzmaurice, 'get into my office now!'

He sat down on his green leather seat as Mr Wilson and Ms Pike entered sheepishly and stood before the desk.

'Well, you knuckleheaded nitwits,' snarled Mr Fitzmaurice, 'in the last few days I've asked you to steal for me a white Persian cat and an ostrich, and what have you brought me?'

'A hamster and a guinea pig?' ventured Mr Wilson.

'Shut up!' roared Mr Fitzmaurice. 'I'll tell you what you've brought me – nothing but grief!' He calmed himself and smoothed down his silk tie. 'The hamster and the guinea pig are nice – in fact, they are lovely and cuddly and very nice – but they are most definitely NOT a white Persian cat and an ostrich.'

'With respect, sir,' said Ms Pike, 'we fought off many foes and were chased by dozens of dangerous dogs to get that hamster and guinea pig.'

'Claptrap and codswallop!' bellowed Mr Fitzmaurice. 'You bought them both in the pet shop – I found the receipt in their cage!'

Mr Wilson and Ms Pike looked even more sheepish. It was true – when they couldn't catch the cat or the ostrich, Mr Wilson had panicked and caught the bus to the pet shop. Now they glanced at each other and then looked down at the expensive rug that covered the floor. 'I'm sorry, sir,' said Mr Wilson, his eyes firmly on the patterned rug, 'we could only afford to buy small animals. I wanted to buy you something more exotic, like a bearded lizard or a tarantula spider, but–'

Roger Fitzmaurice's hands shot involuntarily to his mouth as he stifled a shriek, his eyes wide in momentary terror. 'Mr Wilson!' whispered Ms Pike, 'Do shut up! You know the master is terrified of creepy crawlies!'

Mr Fitmaurice took several deep, shaky breaths before he continued. 'Well, you dunderheaded dimwits,' he said calmly, 'you now have a chance to redeem yourselves. As you know, apart from *(ugh!)* disgusting insects, I love all animals. I especially love the exotic, the unusual, the rare … and the downright indescribable. That's why I want you to kidnap me THIS!'

He held up the front cover of the *Clobberstown Bugle,* and Mr Wilson and Ms Pike leaned in to look at the photo of a very hairy Sam.

'Let me get this straight, sir,' said Mr Wilson, staring at the picture. 'You want us to dog-nap a little girl dressed up as a dog?'

'That's no little girl, you pudding-headed pea-brain!' shrieked Mr Fitzmaurice. 'That is a talking dog. I simply must have it for my collection.'

Ms Pike took out a notepad and a pencil. 'Where does this little girl, pardon me, talking dog live, sir?'

'I haven't the foggiest idea,' said Mr Fitzmaurice. 'But I do know where that incredible creature will be tonight – it is appearing on the television show *Bryan Hoolihan's Midweek Madness*.' He checked his watch. 'That show finishes at eight o'clock. If you two lame-brains are waiting at the stage door of the TV studio at quarter past, you won't have to look for this marvelous mutt – he, she or it will stroll straight into your arms.'

'And what about the dog's friend?' said Ms Wilson, pointing to the photo where Ajay was standing.

'I couldn't care less about humans,' said Mr Fitzmaurice. 'Crack him on the cranium with a crate of crisps for all I care. I JUST WANT THAT DOG!'

'Yes, sir, Mr Fitzmaurice, sir,' said Mr Wilson and Ms Pike together as they backed out of the room.

'You know, Mr Wilson,' said Ms Pike quietly, 'for somebody whose alter ego is Jolly Roger, Mr Fitzmaurice doesn't tend to be very jolly.'

'No,' agreed Mr Wilson, 'he's not very jolly at all.'

Mr Fitzmaurice stared at the photo of Sam in the paper. *Oh yes*, he thought, *you will make a fine addition to my animal collection. If you survive the first day, of course ...*

CHAPTER NINE
HOT DIGITAL DOG

At seven o'clock that evening, Sam, Ajay, Nanny Gigg and Bruno arrived at the studio in a huge stretch limousine that the TV production company had layed on for them. None of them had ever been in a limo before and they marvelled at the plush white leather interior, the crystal-clear sound system, and the little fridge that was full of fizzy drinks.

The driver wore a black peaked cap and was delighted to be bringing Sam to the studio. 'I couldn't believe it when I was the one chosen,' he gushed at Sam as he held the back door of the limo open for her outside the wonky front gate of Clobberstown Lodge. 'I mean, it's not every day you get to drive around an internet sensation! My kids were watching your MyTube video over and over again last night. They can't get enough of it!'

Bruno snorted. 'Heh. Hear that, sis? You're an internet frustration! Haw-haw!'

'Don't mind him, luvvy,' said Nanny Gigg. 'You and Ajay just sit back and enjoy the ride.' She leaned in close to Sam. 'And remember, tomorrow that Train Stop 5000 will be fully charged and you can be you again.'

So Sam did sit back, and she and Ajay both enjoyed the ride through Clobberstown, where the long, sparkling white car got loads of admiring glances from pedestrians all the way to the TV studio. There was a huge poster of Bryan Hoolihan at the studio gate that read '*Watch Bryan Hoolihan's Midweek Madness!*' On the poster, Bryan Hoolihan had a speech bubble above his head that made him look like he was saying his famous catchphrase: 'Call me Hooley!'

The limo pulled up at the studio door and the driver hopped out and opened the back door for the passengers. 'Best of luck, young lady,' he said as Sam got out. 'Here's a little something for Doggie Dinners from me and the kids.' He pushed an envelope into her paw. *More money*, Sam thought. *This is getting ridiculous!*

The door was opened by a smiling floor manager who introduced herself as Lucy, and, after many warm welcomes and hand (or paw) shakes all round, she showed Nanny Gigg and Bruno to their seats in the audience and brought Sam and Ajay backstage to the makeup department. The two friends sat up in high seats with black cloths covering their clothes (or in Sam's case, her fur) as the makeup people and hairdressers fussed around them. They couldn't put makeup on Sam because of the fur, so they satisfied themselves with putting curlers and ribbons into her fuzzy hair. Ajay, however, insisted on getting a full face of makeup, including blue eyeshadow and a roaring red shade of lipstick.

They were still sitting in the chairs, admiring themselves in the lightbulb-encircled mirrors, when Bryan Hoolihan himself strode in, his hand thrust out for a good shake. 'Call me Hooley!' he boomed in a very dramatic voice while vigorously pumping Sam's paw. 'You must be young Sam. Oh! Your costume is A-MAY-ZING! Do you know, if I didn't know better, I'd think you were actually a dog?'

He turned to Ajay. 'And who have we here? Oh, holy mother of Molly! That's, eh, that's a lovely paint job you've had done to you there.' With a big fixed smile he looked at the makeup people and hissed quietly, 'Would you get some baby wipes and mop that load of muck off his face? He can't go on camera like that – he looks like my great-auntie Eileen!' He turned back to the kids. 'SO good to meet you both. I'll see ye on set! Toodles!'

Sam and Ajay were the third set of guests on the show, after a model called Ivanka Petrovovovovich who was talking about her new book, *Ivanka's Dust and Carpet Fluff Diet*, and an actor called Brad O'Brady who starred in the daytime soap *Liffey Life*.

As Brad was finishing his chat with Bryan Hoolihan, Lucy the floor manager hustled Sam and Ajay to the curtain at the side of the set. 'Right, kids,' she said, 'the commercials are up next. We'll get you on set and miked up while they're on.'

There was applause from the audience as Brad O'Brady's bit ended, and then a bell rang. 'We're clear,' whispered Lucy into her headset. She brought Sam and Ajay on stage, where they sat on a long, pink sofa across from Bryan Hoolihan.

'Don't be nervous,' said Bryan. 'Sure it's only a bit of fun.'

A sound girl quickly clipped a microphone to Ajay's shirt collar and to Sam's dog collar and backed off stage. 'All right,' said Lucy, 'we're back in three, two, one ...'

A sign saying APPLAUSE lit up over the set, so the audience did what it suggested and clapped, hooted and squealed with delight. Nanny Gigg waved at Sam excitedly, her false teeth slipping loose as she tried to whistle, and even Bruno, although looking bored, managed a slow handclap.

'Welcome back!' said Bryan. 'Next up we have a heart-warming story of a young girl who has pledged to dress up as a dog for four whole days for her favourite animal charity, and in the process has become an overnight internet smash – it's Clobbertown's own Sam Hannigan. Call me Hooley, Sam!'

'Call me Hooley!' repeated the audience, cheering and whooping.

'Hi, eh, Hooley,' said Sam.

'Well, I've got to say, your costume is A-MAY-ZING. Isn't it, ladies and gentlemen? What do you think of that costume, guys and gals?' The audience whooped and clapped their appreciation. 'Now, did you make that yourself or did you buy it in a shop? And if you bought it in a shop, you have to tell me which one – you just have to.'

'I made it with my friend, Ajay,' said Sam. She didn't like to tell a fib, but she couldn't tell the whole world – or at least the whole of Ireland – about Daddy Mike's Brain Swap 3000. She was glad her face was covered in fur and nobody could see her blushing.

Ajay's face was still covered in quite a thick layer of makeup, so blushing wasn't an issue for him. Unfortunately, speaking was an issue for him. As soon as the red light switched on over the camera to let them know they were live on air, Ajay froze with terror.

Sam looked over at Ajay, hoping he'd jump in on the conversation, but when she saw he was paralysed with stage fright, she kept going. 'Yes,' she said, 'Ajay and I made it from, em, fake fur left over from the last school fashion show and some fake plastic teeth we bought in the joke shop. Ajay's mum helped with the sewing, she's brilliant at sewing. Hi, Ajay's mum!' She waved at the camera and hoped that Ajay's mum wasn't watching. She was actually rubbish at sewing.

'Now, Sam,' said Bryan, 'tell me all about your favourite charity, Doggie Dinners.'

'It's Dinners for Dogs, Bryan – sorry, Mr Hooley – sorry, Hooley.' She let out a barky cough. 'It provides stray, homeless and abandoned dogs with food and a place to sleep. Just until they get back on their paws.'

'Sounds wonderful,' said Bryan. 'I love dogs, they are just A-MAY-ZING.'

'And it's not just for dogs,' said Sam. 'It's for all abandoned animals – cats, birds, monkeys, fish, lizards, snakes, insects – we aim to give a good home to them all.'

'You are two wonderful human beings, just WON-DER-FUL,' said Bryan. 'Now tell me, Sam, you're wearing that dog costume twenty-four hours a day – does it get itchy?'

'Not at all,' said Sam brightly. 'It's almost like a second skin at this stage. I sometimes forget I've got it on!'

'Fair play to you, FAIR PLAY. And if our audience or the viewers at home want to donate to Dinners for Doggies, how can they do that?' smiled Bryan.

'They can send money to our school, St Gobnet's National School in Clobberstown,' said Sam, 'or they can send it to Clobberstown Lodge, Clobberstown Avenue, also in, em, Clobberstown.' Sam thought she had said the word 'Clobberstown' quite enough for one day.

'That's fantastic. FAN-TAS-TIC. Well, the best of luck with it. I hope you raise a HUGE amount of money and that the doggies ALL get their dinner. That's Sam Hannigan and Ajay Patel – lovely talking to you, Ajay – the internet sensations who are collecting cash in canine costume for Doggie Dinners. We'll see you after the break!'

The audience applauded and a bell sounded. 'You were brillant, kids,'
said Bryan as a makeup person dabbed at his face with a small sponge.
'You're naturals on TV, NAT-U-RALS. And SUCH a good idea! Leave
your details with Lucy, won't you? Let me know if you've any other great
ideas in the future!'

Lucy brought them off the set and back behind the curtain, then went
off to fetch Nanny Gigg and Bruno from where they were sitting in the
audience. Nanny Gigg blew kisses to Bryan Hoolihan as she left her seat.

'Well, that wasn't so bad,' whispered Ajay. 'I thought we got through
that quite well.'

'WE??' said Sam. 'What do you mean *WE??* I did all the talking!'

'Well done, both of you,' said Lucy, joining them again with Nanny
Gigg and Bruno in tow. 'Now, we'll have to get you to leave by the back

door – there's quite a crowd of fans and press waiting for you at the front.'

'Good idea,' said Nanny Gigg. 'I wouldn't like to see my precious grand-dog-ter getting hurt in a media frenzy!'

'I've radioed the limo to pull around to the back,' said Lucy, opening the door and peeping out. 'Ah! Here it is now!'

The big white limo pulled up to the stage door. 'Go, go, go!' said Lucy, and Sam and Ajay made a run for it. Sam bounded into the back seat of the limo, but when Ajay reached the car door, it slammed shut in his face. There was a screech of tyres and the limo drove off – with Sam inside!

Ajay stood surrounded by a cloud of dust, watching the car as it disappeared into the distance. Bruno and Nanny Gigg, having said their goodbyes to Lucy the floor manager (who went back inside to, em, manage the floors), joined Ajay on the footpath.

'Where's the limo?' asked Bruno.

'Never mind the limo,' said Nanny Gigg. **'WHERE'S MY SAM?!'**

THE MIS-ADVENTURES OF MR WILSON & Ms PIKE

CHAPTER TEN
CAPTIVE CANINE

Sam woke up the next morning and, as usual, her paws immediately went up to her face. *Yup. Still a dog.*

But, hold on a minute, this wasn't her bed! Come to think of it, this wasn't even her bed*room*! She opened her eyes to find herself lying on a dirty, hair-covered blanket on the floor of a huge, ramshackle warehouse. In the distance she could hear what sounded like machinery creaking and wheezing. The ceiling of the tumbledown warehouse was high and there were holes in the rusty corrugated sheets of roof metal through which she could see the morning light. She looked left and right, her long ears flopping from side to side. Where the blinking barnacles *was* she?

Suddenly, the morning air around Sam's head started to turn a little green in colour. Her doggy nose twitched and then started to shudder as the most horrible smell she had ever smelled in her entire life wafted over towards where she lay.

Sam jumped to her four feet and, without being able to help herself, started to growl.

'Hey,' said a chirpy voice, 'I hope that growl's not for me!'

From around a rusty pillar trotted a very small dog. He was jet-black in colour, with short hair and small legs that didn't look strong enough to support the weight of his long body. He was so close to the ground that his lengthy ears dragged along beside him, raising up small clouds of dust. There seemed to be, as he scuttled over to Sam, another cloud hanging around this dog: an invisible cloud of SMELLY GAS.

It's a little-known fact that dogs' noses are ten thousand times more sensitive to smell than human noses. *Ten thousand times*. So when Sam's nose fully caught that horrible, disgusting PONG, she had a very hard time forcing herself not to high-tail it down to the other end of the warehouse. After a couple of seconds of trying to control her urge to run, her well-mannered side won out and she decided to stay put and greet this stinky stranger.

Sam coughed and put her paw to her nose. 'Excuse me. Of course

I wasn't growling at you, I just was growling at another– Hold on a minute. I can UNDERSTAND WHAT YOU'RE SAYING!'

'Naturally,' said the small dog. 'I'm a dog, you're a dog, we all speak the same language.'

'Holy moley,' said Sam. 'I've been a dog for nearly four days now and I never thought to try speaking to another one – this is A-MAY-ZING!'

'Huh?' said the small dog, who had obviously never watched *Bryan Hoolihan's Midweek Madness*. 'My name's Stephen, but everyone calls me Stinker.'

'No kidding,' said Sam, still holding her paw to her nose. 'I'm Sam.'

Without thinking, they both went around to each other's rear end and had a little sniff.

'Okay,' said Sam, 'where are we?'

'Oh,' said Stinker, 'you don't know?' He led Sam to the huge metal door of the warehouse; light streamed in around the sides and at the bottom.

'It's locked,' said Sam, pushing against the door with her snout.

'No prob-*lemmo*,' said Stinker, and, crouching even lower to the ground, squeezed his small body underneath the door. A couple of seconds later the door swung open. 'There's a switch to open it on the wall outside,' he said. 'It's quite high up, but I can reach it.' Sam looked up at the switch as she walked through the door. It was about thirty centimetres off the ground.

'This is where we are,' said Stinker, pointing up at the wall of the warehouse with his snout. Sam gaped at a big poster that hung over the door. 'Can't read it myself,' said Stinker. 'It's all in human.'

Sam could read it. 'Don't worry, I'm actually human – I can read human.' She told Stinker all about the Brain Swap 3000 and all about Barker being mistreated and how she was now stuck being a dog.

'Hold on, you're really a human and not a dog at all?' asked Stinker, looking her up and down. 'But you were nice to that poor dog Barker, so that makes you more dog than human in my book.'

'Thanks,' said Sam, 'I *think* ...'

Sam looked up at the poster. It had a familiar, colourful, smiling face on it – *it was Jolly Roger, the dog biscuit guy!* The poster read 'Welcome to the Jolly Roger™ Dog Biscuit Factory – the Home of Jolly Roger Dog Biscuits.' Underneath these words was a picture of Jolly Roger himself holding one of his dog biscuits up to a happy-looking dog and saying, 'Yarr! Your Dog Will Love 'Em!'

'That dog in the picture was called Flossie,' said Stinker, as he led Sam across a dusty courtyard to a large cement-walled building. 'She tried to escape, and, well, let's just say it didn't go so good for her.'

'Escape?' said Sam. 'Escape from what?'

'From this,' said Stinker, and he led Sam into the cement building through a big doorway with steel shutters that looked like a gaping mouth.

The noise inside the cement building was deafening. It was the sound of clanking, clanging, clunking machinery, but those metal sounds were mixed together with other sounds – noises that sounded to Sam like muffled barks, neighs, squawks and whinnies.

Along the far wall of the room was a line of big metal machines that went all the way up to the ceiling. Each of them had exposed cogs whirring around and pistons pumping up and down. Conveyor belts emerged from two of the machines, and bright red boxes slid along them.

In the centre of the building was a big vat, made of huge sheets of steel held together with metal rivets the size of dinner plates. Steam drifted from the top of the vat and a green-coloured goo burbled over the side in places.

'What's in that?' asked Sam, even though she was half afraid to find out the answer.

Stinker sighed. 'Sam,' he said, 'look closer at the machines over there. Can you see? Those huge machines make Jolly Roger Dog Biscuits, but they aren't powered by electricity.'

'What are they powered by then?' asked Sam. Her fur was getting itchy and the doggy hackles at the back of her neck were rising. She didn't like this place.

'Look at the big air holes in the sides of the machinery. Look right into them,' said Stinker. 'What can you see?'

'ANIMALS!' said Sam. 'I see animals! I see dogs, cats, ponies, donkeys, horses, monkeys, parrots, budgies, monkeys, camels, and – are they hamsters? They are all inside the machines!'

As Sam gawked at the machines, a troupe of small brown monkeys with chains around their ankles led a sad-looking, golden-coloured carthorse to the end of the conveyor belts. They listlessly started to load the red boxes onto the back of the four-wheel cart the enormous carthorse was pulling. Sam gasped.

Stinker shook his small head, his long ears raising up dust from the dirty floor. 'They are made to walk on treadmills, on big hamster wheels – all to keep the machinery going. Those poor creatures save old Roger loads of money on electricity by making the machines run by paw- and hoof-power.'

'They're made to do it? They don't have a choice?' asked Sam, aghast.

'Hah! Choice?' laughed Stinker grimly. 'These poor critters are no better than slaves. They are made to work, fed very little, and when they're worn out and can't work any more' – he nodded his head toward the massive vat in the middle of the room – 'they end up in there.'

'They go into the vat? Why?' asked Sam.

'Why? To be made into dog biscuits, of course! Old Jolly Roger doesn't waste anything. When slave animals here have outlived their usefulness, they are chucked into the vat, boiled up and melted down, and then the goo they become is pumped down those pipes' – Stinker pointed with his snout at three dripping pipes leading from the vat, then he turned his nose towards the machines at the far wall – 'and all the way into those machines, where the goo is mixed, shaped and baked and comes out the other end as Jolly Roger Dog Biscuits!'

Sam stared at the vat and gulped. The poor, poor animals ...

CHAPTER ELEVEN
A DOG-GONE SHAME

Ajay walked slowly to school the next morning. He had big black rings under his eyes from lack of sleep. After leaving the TV station, he had spent a couple of hours in Clobberstown Garda Station reporting Sam's abduction and talking to the guards, then he, Nanny Gigg and Bruno had gone back to Clobberstown Lodge to try to figure out who might have taken Sam and why. Ajay's dad had picked him up at one o'clock in the morning after his taxi-driving shift, so poor Ajay hadn't had much sleep.

He shuffled along the path outside the school with his head down and didn't notice Martha Maguire and Abbie Cuffe until he nearly walked into them. Martha was holding up the front page of that day's *Clobberstown Bugle*. Ajay lifted his head and looked at it: 'DOG GONE – INTERNET AND TV SENSATION SAM HANNIGAN ABDUCTED!' There was a photo of Sam, this time as her real self, with her human red hair and freckles, and beside it a smaller repeat of the photo of Sam as a dog.

'*What* are you doing at school, Ajay?' demanded Martha. 'Why aren't you out looking for Sam?'

'I didn't know you cared so much about her,' said Ajay.

'Yeah, well …' started Martha, but Abbie jumped in, 'We know Sam's really a dog. That's not a costume she's wearing. She's a dog, she's changed into a dog, she's really a dog.'

'Wow,' said Ajay, 'you guys are ker-azy. Sam can't be a dog! She's in a costume! Collecting for Doggie Dinners!'

'I thought it was Dinners for Dogs,' said Martha. She put down the newspaper. 'Look. We *know* she's a real dog. We don't know how it happened and we don't really care. But Sam is a St Gobnet's student and a member of the Cú Chulainn Academy and nobody, and I mean *nobody*, gets to mess with us. And besides that, her brother is a total babe.'

Abbie looked at Ajay and rolled her eyes. Ajay smiled a bit, despite himself.

'Okay, okay,' he said. 'You're right, she's a real dog.' He told them all about the Brain Swap 3000 and how Sam turned into next door's dog Barker to play a trick on Barker's owner, and how the gun had run out of charge and how she was stuck being a dog until today. *Actually*, he thought, *in all the excitement last night, I forgot to check the Brain Swap 3000 – it must be fully charged by now!*

'So, what can we do?' asked Martha.

'Well, there's not much we *can* do,' said Ajay. 'The gardaí are out looking for her, and they told me to go to school as normal and wait for developments.'

'Wait for developments?' said Martha. 'No way, Ajay. We're going to help find her ourselves. Watch this.'

They had just gotten up to the gate of the school when Martha let out a huge, anguished wail. 'A-huk-ayaaaaaaaaaahhhh!' she cried. 'I'm so upset over Sam Hannigan, I can't go to school!'

Ms Hennigan, the principal, ran over to the gate with the caretaker Ogg in tow. 'Oh, you poor thing,' she said. 'You must be dreadfully upset! Will I call your mum to collect you?'

'No,' cried Martha. 'That won't be neccessary. Ajay and Abbie will take me home. They're upset too.' She elbowed Abbie in the ribs and both Abbie and Ajay started to sob.

'Of course you all are upset, everyone is. I want you three to go home and have a nice cup of tea to settle your nerves.'

'Thanks, Ms Hennigan,' said Martha brightly, and the three of them turned and walked back down School Road as quickly as they could, sobbing as they went.

Ogg looked after them as they went. *Humph*, he thought. *Ms Hennigan is a big softie. I don't think they were really crying at all ...*

As soon as they got around the corner and were out of earshot, the sobbing stopped. 'Okay, so what's the plan?' asked Martha.

'Only one place to go,' said Ajay. 'Clobberstown Lodge! But we need to swing by my house on the way.'

CHAPTER TWELVE
A MALODOROUS MUTT

'Oh. My. Dog,' said Sam, staring at the vat where so many poor animals had met their end.

'Oh. My. Dog. *Biscuits*,' said Stinker. '*Buy Jolly Rogers, Your Dog Will Love 'Em.*'

'Yarr ...' said Sam quietly. She was thinking queasily and uneasily about all the dog biscuits that Bruno had force-fed her over the years.

'Yarr, indeed,' said a voice from behind. Sam spun around on her paws. Looking up, she saw a tall, slender man with a pencil-thin moustache and an ill-fitting wig. He wore a grey suit with a red tie and what looked like an oversized handkerchief in his breast pocket. 'Allow me to introduce myself. My name is Roger Fitzmaurice.'

'Jolly Roger! The guy from the TV ads!' Sam said without thinking.

'Ahh,' said Mr Fitzmaurice, one side of his thin mouth stretched up into a crooked smile. 'So it *is* true, you *are* a talking dog!'

Sam gasped. She looked around for Stinker, but he had mysteriously vanished. For a small dog with tiny legs, thought Sam, he can certainly move quickly.

'Oh my goodness,' said Mr Fitzmaurice. 'What is that smell?' He took the red hanky out of his pocket and held it to his nose – to Sam it looked like the pirate bandana that Jolly Roger wore on the advert. 'I certainly hope it isn't you making that smell,' he said with a sneer. 'I'd hate to have to throw you into the vat before I got my money's worth out of you.'

He smiled his crooked half-smile at Sam. 'You see, my dear doggie, I want to make you a star. I want you to be the lead actor in my new series of Jolly Roger™ Dog Biscuit commercials! Can you imagine it? A real-life talking dog, appearing on every television, laptop and tablet in the land, telling dog owners to buy Jolly Roger™ Dog Biscuits for their beloved mutts! What do you say to that?'

'I say forget it, it isn't going to happen,' said Sam. 'There's no way I'm going to help you sell these horrible dog biscuits, especially now that I've seen what goes into them!'

Sam stood up on her hind legs. She was nearly as tall as Mr Fitzmaurice. 'And I'll tell you another thing, Jolly Roger, I'm going to let everyone know about this evil place. I'm going to go to the police and to the Clobberstown Bugle and to Bryan Hoolihan himself, and I'm going to get this place SHUT DOWN!'

Mr Fitzmaurice smiked his half-smirk. 'Wilson! Pike!' he yelled. 'Here! Now!'

Mr Wilson and Ms Pike scurried up from the depths of the factory to stand beside their boss. 'Here!' shouted Mr Wilson. 'We! Are!' continued Ms Pike.

'What took you so long?' snarled Mr Fitzmaurice. 'Take this ... dog ... away and teach it some manners.'

'You mean, like, table manners?' asked Mr Wilson.

'Ps and Qs?' asked Ms Pike.

'I mean the type of manners that are taught with this,' growled Mr Fitzmaurice, holding up a long leather riding crop.

'Oh, Mr Fitzmaurice,' said Ms Pike, 'that would hurt the poor little thing!'

'Please don't ask us to hurt her, Jolly Rog– I mean, Mr Fitzmaurice, sir,' said Mr Wilson, looking as though he was about to cry.

'You dim-witted dumb-bells!' started Mr Fitzmaurice, but that was as far as he got into that particular insult, because at that second a small, tiny-legged dog appeared from behind a pillar and did what he did best – he made a stink. Stinker let go with an ear-shattering, eggy-smelling

PpAAAAaarrRRRrrpppPPPppp-pPPpp!!

that made the walls of the factory building shake and made Mr Wilson and Ms Pike's eyes water. Mr Fitzmaurice covered his nose and mouth with the red pirate bandana.

'Get. That. Malodorous. Mutt!!' Mr Fitzmaurice managed to choke out between taking extremely small breaths. The air was almost glowing green with the putrid smell – a cross between blocked drains, overflowing toilets and the bins on a hot summer's day.

As Mr Wilson and Ms Pike, their faces green with revulsion at the stench, slowly walked towards Sam, Stinker ran around behind Mr Fitzmaurice's legs and started barking. 'What's up with that dunderheaded dachshund? What's he barking for?' gasped Mr Fitzmaurice. 'Sam!' shouted Stinker. 'If the car you're in on the way to the vet breaks down, what do you do?'

'You give it a push!' said Sam, and, rearing up, she jumped up and pushed Mr Fitzmaurice in the chest with her two front paws.

Mr Fitzmaurice tripped over Stinker's small body and went flying backwards, landing on his backside. His wig fell off and his pirate bandana fluttered through the air after him.

Mr Wilson and Ms Pike rushed to help Mr Fitzmaurice up, but he shook them off. 'Never mind me,' he shouted. 'Get that dog!'

But Sam had run out of the evil factory building, past paddocks, stockades and cages that held a great many animals of all different varieties and breeds, all of them looking underfed and miserable. They started whooping and howling as she scampered past. Sam was closely followed by Stinker, who was holding something black and shiny in his mouth. They raced around a corner and behind some storage sheds. Sam peeped from behind the wall. 'How do we get out of here, Stinker?' she asked. 'All I can see are high walls and electric fences right around this compound!'

'I have an idea,' said Stinker in a muffled voice. He tossed the object he had been carrying in his mouth onto the ground. 'You could always phone for help.'

'Is that,' asked Sam in an incredulous voice, 'Roger Fitzmaurice's mobile phone?'

'Yup,' said Stinker. 'I bet he won't be so *Jolly* when he realises it's missing!'

'I could call Ajay! And Nanny Gigg! And Bruno too, I suppose,' said Sam happily. 'Oh, but there's a problem – I can't punch in the numbers with these paws.'

'No worries,' said Stinker. '*You* may not be able to punch in the numbers, but I know a whole troupe of monkeys who can!'

CHAPTER THIRTEEN
DUCK RESCUES DOG!

Ajay, Martha and Abbie flew through the wonky gate and ran up the path to the front door of Clobberstown Lodge. Ajay reached for the doorbell but pulled his hand back – the doorbell, like most of the bits and pieces in Clobberstown Lodge, looked broken.

'We could try knocking?' said Martha. But none of them got a chance to put their knuckles into action, because at that moment the door swung open to reveal Nanny Gigg with her mobile phone clamped to her ear, pulling on her coat with her one free hand.

'AJAY!' she cried. 'Sam, luvvy, Ajay's at the door with Martha and Abbie! Yes, *that* Martha and Abbie. They've all come to help, luvvy! Sit tight, we'll be there soon!'

Nanny Gigg finished the call and then looked at the three astonished kids, her eyes wide, 'Sam's been dog-napped by Roger Fitzmaurice!'

'*Jolly* Roger Fitzmaurice?' said Martha.

'The dog biscuit king?' asked Abbie.

'That's the one,' said Nanny Gigg. 'They're keeping her in the dog biscuit factory at the other side of Clobberstown. We've got to hurry – she says they want to turn her into dog biscuits!'

'I'll call my dad,' said Ajay. 'He can come around with the taxi!'

'Why wait for a taxi,' said Bruno, appearing in the hallway behind Nanny Gigg, 'when we've got our own transport?' He jingled a set of keys. 'Come on – Daddy Mike left us a little something in the inventing shed.'

A few minutes later there was a huge KERR-ASSHHHH! as an enormous amphibious vehicle smashed through the garden fence at the back of the house, reducing it to matchwood. The gigantic green 'duck' truck had a curved front that looked like the prow of a boat, bright-orange life rings up the sides, and six big wheels. At the steering wheel sat Nanny Gigg, wearing a Sherlock Holmes–style deerstalker hat and a pair of leather-trimmed goggles.

'I remember when Daddy Mike built this,' Nanny Gigg shouted back to Ajay, Bruno, Martha and Abbie, who were sitting behind her, 'he used to drive me up to Glendalough and we'd steer old Big Bertha here into the lake and boat around for a couple of hours fishing for trout. Happy days.'

Ajay shifted in his seat, holding on tight to a little plastic box in his hand and making sure the lid with the air holes didn't come off.

'This thing can go in the water?' asked Abbie.

'Of course it can!' shouted Nanny Gigg over the engine noise.

'It's a floating-boating monster truck,' said Bruno. 'Daddy Mike was a genius, you know.'

Abbie and Martha fluttered their eyelashes at Bruno and giggled. Oh, please, thought Ajay.

Bruno winked at the girls. 'My old grandpa could invent anything – including this little beauty!' He held up the Brain Swap 3000. 'And it's all charged up and ready to rock and roll!'

Nanny Gigg swung the floating-boating monster truck around onto Clobberstown Road and straight into a traffic jam. 'Traffic?' she roared, nearly losing her false teeth. 'I'm fit to spit!' She shook her small, wrinkly fist at the tiny blue car blocking Big Bertha's way. 'Move it, you doze-bucket!'

The traffic cleared when they turned onto School Road, and it was plain sailing from there to the other side of town. Ajay wondered why so many people were cheering at them and waving as they went, then he realised why: *They think we're a Viking tour!*

When they reached the gates of the Jolly Roger Dog Biscuit factory, Nanny Gigg pressed her left foot onto the brake and pulled Big Bertha in alongside the kerb on the other side of the road. They stared over at the factory gates; they were tall and wooden and looked very strong. The walls that surrounded the compound were twenty feet high and topped with sharp-looking barbed wire. A security man with dark glasses and a walkie-talkie stood in front of the gates, staring at Nanny Gigg and the kids in their floating-boating monster truck. He raised the walkie-talkie to his mouth.

'Time to save Sam,' said Nanny Gigg quietly. 'Hold on tight, kids.'

She put her right foot on the accelerator pedal and floored it. The truck's engine had been idling and ticking away faintly, but now it roared into life with a monstrous VA-VA-VARROOOOOOMMMMMM! Nanny Gigg wrenched the steering wheel around and Big Bertha sprang on its big wheels straight toward the gate.

The security man gaped at the massive truck heading directly for him and immediately dropped the walkie-talkie and dived for safety.

Big Bertha hit the gates at full speed, knocking them off their hinges with a thunderous sound of breaking wood and twisting metal. The truck ran over the fallen gates, marking them with giant rubber tyre marks as it burst into the factory compound. Sirens started to wail with an ARRRRUUUUUGGGA ARRRRUUUUUGGGA sound.

Big Bertha skidded to a full stop just inside the gates, sending up clouds of dust and jerking the kids suddenly forward against their safety belts. Nanny Gigg stood up in the driver's seat and peered around the factory compound. *Where is Sam?*

Martha started to ask what they were going to do next, but her words were drowned out by the sudden cacophony of galloping hooves, paws and claws as scores of animals spotted the ruined gates and took their long-awaited opportunity to escape. They hooted, barked and howled for joy as they ran past Big Bertha and through the gates to freedom. Many of the larger beasts were helping the smaller animals, and the monkeys sat on the back of some of the bigger dogs, riding them like jockeys.

When the escaping animals were all through the gates and the noise died down, Nanny Gigg started to shout, 'Sam! Where are you?'

She was joined by Ajay, who hopped down from Big Bertha holding a little plastic box and whistling, 'Sam! Here, girl!'

Dogs' noses may be more sensitive than humans' noses, but dogs' ears are in a class of their own – not only can dogs hear much better then humans, their ears are mobile and flexible and can move around like little satellite dishes to seek out and track sounds. So when Sam heard the sound of Ajay's whistle, her furry ears perked up, followed the sound and – despite Stinker's protestations – let out a huge

HOW-HOW-HoOooOoooOo ooWWwWWWwLLLlLLl!

and ran pell-mell in the direction the whistle came from.

Unfortunately she ran straight into Mr Wilson, who, remembering his school sports days, rugby-tackled her and held her tight by the back legs while Ms Pike attached a chain leash to her collar and quickly slipped a muzzle onto her snout. 'Sorry, doggy,' she said apologetically. 'Nothing personal, I'm just following orders.'

'Let me go!' shouted Sam through the wire mesh of her muzzle.

'I'm afraid that won't be possible,' said Roger Fitzmaurice, striding towards them and grabbing Sam's leash from Ms Pike. 'I don't care if you're really a human – you're MY mutt now.'

Suddenly there was a roar of engines and a screech of brakes. Roger, Ms Pike, Mr Wilson and Sam found themselves surrounded by a cloud of dust. They also found themselves surrounded by Ajay, Bruno, Martha, Abbie and Nanny Gigg.

'That's no mutt,' bellowed Nanny Gigg at the top of her voice, 'that's my granddaughter!'

'Get back,' hissed Roger Fitzmaurice, 'or this cretinous canine goes into the vat.' He raised his voice. 'In fact, ALL the animals will go into the vat!'

Sam twisted around on her leash. She slipped her snout out of the muzzle and bit Roger hard on the hand.

He shrieked, dropped the leash and jammed his fist into his mouth. 'You horrible hound!' he cried.

'Bite me!' shouted Sam and started barking. She was answered by a series of higher-pitched barks that seemed to come from low down near the ground. Stinker appeared from behind a yellow skip, and as he trotted closer to the group they raised their hands to their noses to block out the smell that he brought along with him.

He also brought along with him the huge carthorse that had been tethered to the four-wheel cart. 'Sam!' yelled Stinker. 'I got the monkeys to unhook Old Charlie here from the cart! He says he wants to help!'

Old Charlie started to whinny and bray loudly. Ajay, Nanny Gigg and the gang cheered, while Roger Fitzmaurice and his hench-people backed away with frightened looks on their faces.

'Bruno!' shouted Sam. 'Quick! Brain-swap me with the horse!'

Bruno smiled broadly and raised the Brain Swap 3000. 'You got it, sis!'

He aimed the device at Sam the dog's head and pulled the trigger. A sudden rush of wind blew through the yard, followed by a *schlorpy, schloooorpy* sound, and then a bright beam of blue light shot out of the trumpet end of Daddy Mike's marvellous invention. Barker hit the floor, then jumped straight back up again and started barking happily. The dog ran to Ajay and licked his hand. Ajay happily petted her. Bruno looked at the readout on the Brain Swap 3000. It read 'Power: 95%, Contents: 100%'. 'Woo-hoo!' whooped Bruno. 'It worked!'

He spun around and aimed at the horse, pulling the trigger as he did so. The rush of wind was stronger this time and the schlorpy, schloooopy sound was louder. The horse immediately stopped whinnying and turned his massive head towards Roger Fitzmaurice.

'Fitzmaurice,' roared Sam, her mind now inhabiting the enormous carthorse, 'you have mistreated the animals here long enough! You will mistreat them no more! The animals say NEIGH!' She reared up on her hind legs and Roger Fitzmaurice, dodging her flailing hooves, fell on his backside in the dust.

'Wilson! Pike!' he cried. 'Get that gun!'

Ms Pike and Mr Wilson looked at each other in bewilderment and then, in panic, made a run at Bruno, who was holding the Brain Swap 3000. Green smoke swirled lazily out of its trumpet end. Bruno spotted the hench-people at the last second and threw the gun to Martha, who used her Irish dancing skills to deftly sidestep the pair of ham-fisted hench-people.

Sam neighed loudly and Stinker leapt into Abbie's arms. Sam boomed out in her deep carthorse voice, 'Abbie! The dog's name is Stinker – if you want to displease, just give him a squeeze!'

Abbie, who also had a bullying older brother at home who was a dab hand with an aqua-blaster got the idea straight away. She turned Stinker around so his head was under her armpit and his doggy bottom was facing their foes. Stinker barked three times – 'Go! Go! Go!' – and Abbie squeezed down on his doggy tummy with her elbow, like she was attempting to play a particularly smelly set of bagpipes. With an enormous

PAAAARRRRRPPPPP

noise, a huge cloud of evil gas erupted from the tiny dog's rear end.

Mr Wilson and Ms Pike were immediately stopped in their tracks by the foul, noxious smell and fell to their knees holding their noses.

Roger Fitzmaurice jumped to his feet and, taking out his pirate bandana and wrapping it around his mouth – and, more importantly, his nose – proceeded to round on Martha. 'If I can't have the talking dog, I'll have that extraordinary Brain Swap gun,' he said to Martha menacingly. 'Gimme!'

A group of security guards rounded a corner and hastened towards their boss, each holding a walkie-talkie in one hand and using their other hand to hold their noses.

'Not so fast!' cried Ajay, opening up the small plastic box he had been carrying with him. 'Mr Fitzmaurice, or can I call you Jolly Roger? I'd like you to say hello to my little friend, Tadhg … Tadhg the Tarantula!'

'NO!' shouted Mr Fitzmaurice. His voice was so high it sounded like he had been sucking on a helium balloon, 'Don't you DARE! I HATE spiders!'

Ajay picked up Tadhg from the box and threw him at Mr Fitzmaurice. Tadhg landed on Fitzmaurice's chest and crawled up towards his face. Mr Fitzmaurice boggled down at the small, hairy, eight-legged creepy-crawly and let out a high-pitched, helium-fuelled SCRREEEEEECH! In a small voice he whispered, 'Oh, bother,' then his body went rigid with terror and he fell backwards onto the ground like a freshly chopped tree.

Nanny Gigg looked up at Sam the carthorse. 'Sam, luvvy,' she said, winking at her extremely tall granddaughter, 'maybe it'd be a good idea to become human again, you know, before the security guards arrive?'

Sam winked a big-eyelashed, horsey eye back at her granny. 'Sounds good to me,' she said and then turned to Martha. 'Time to make Roger a bit more Jolly.'

Martha nodded and smiled, then aimed the Brain Swap 3000 at the horse and extracted Sam's brain. She quickly turned the device on the unmoving figure of Roger Fitzmaurice and fired. Fitzmaurice's body twitched once where it lay on the ground, and then Roger jumped to his feet. 'Halt!' he shouted to the guards, who were just reaching them. 'Hold your horses!'

'Do not interfere with these kids or this charming old lady,' yelled Sam in a commanding Roger Fitzmaurice voice. 'Sorry for calling you old, Nanny Gigg,' she whispered to her granny. 'I'm pretending to be Roger now.'

'I want all you boys to have a three-week paid holiday, on me, Jolly Roger Fitzmaurice,' continued Sam, holding up Roger's finger in a superior fashion. 'Starting from today!'

The guards looked at one another quizzically and shrugged.

'But before you go,' added Sam, 'I want you to free any of the animals that are still locked up. Got it?'

'We get it, boss!' they cried, and, clapping one another on the back, went off happily to locate keys and unlock locks.

Sam turned to where Mr Wilson and Ms Pike lay on the ground. They were still waving their hands in front of their noses, trying to waft away the smell of Stinker's exceptionally pungent rear-end release. She furrowed Roger's eyebrows and glared at them. 'I want you two dog-napping dunces to take this' – Sam reached into the pocket of Roger's jacket and produced a wallet stuffed with banknotes – 'and go on a long, long vacation.'

Sam tossed the wallet to Mr Wilson, who looked into it with his eyes wide. 'Or perhaps, Ms Pike,' said Mr Wilson slowly, clearing his throat with a short, strangled cough, 'instead of a vacation, we could make it a … a honeymoon?'

Ms Pike took the wallet from Mr Wilson and opened it. 'Oh, Mr Wilson,' she said, her eyes boggling at the cash – there must have been thousands in there! 'I thought you'd never ask!'

They both hopped up off the ground and, with a small wave, scuttled off hand in hand out the gates.

'Now,' said Sam, wiping Roger Fitzmaurice's forehead with the pirate bandana, 'time to go home. Time to be *me* again.'

CHAPTER FOURTEEN
LUCKY DOG! AND CAT! AND DUCK! AND OSTRICH! ETC! ETC!

The morning was sunny and silent, apart from the distant sound of a dog barking. Dust motes circled and danced lazily in the bright beams of sunlight that shone through the bedroom window.

Surrounded by her own comfy pillows, under her own warm duvet, in her own one-size-too-small pyjamas, Sam Hannigan woke up. Out of habit, she lifted her hands to her face. Smooth and hairless, just like it should be. She was just plain old red-headed, frizzy-haired, freckly-faced Sam once more.

She had enjoyed being herself again for these last few weeks. She had also enjoyed painting and repairing Clobberstown Lodge with the help of her new friends Martha and Abbie, and her oldest and bestest friend, Ajay, and her granny and brother.

The money that had been donated to Doggie Dinners (or Dinners for Dogs) had helped pay for the transformation of Clobberstown Lodge into Hannigan's Haven, a sanctuary for all animals, large and small, exotic and ordinary.

Ajay and Bruno had counted up the money that Nanny Gigg had stuffed into kitchen presses, bread bins and cookie jars, and they could not believe how much was sent in. People were still sending money in now, mainly thanks to Sam's triumphant reappearance after her mysterious disappearance. She made the front page of the *Clobberstown Bugle* again, this time without her dog 'costume'. Beside her in the photograph was Roger Fitzmaurice, who, having mostly seen the error of his ways, was holding an enormous cheque for an even more enormous amount of money, made out to Hannigan's Haven. Although Roger had what looked like a smile on his face in the photograph, he did not seem to be entirely jolly – he looked like he was wincing his eyes and grinding his teeth at the same time.

Hannigan's Haven was now home to over fifty animals – they had dogs, cats, mice, an ostrich, two wallabies and several fish, as well as Charlie, the old carthorse. Stinker was also a permanent guest, as was Barker, who had been 'donated' by the Hannigans' next-door neighbour, Mr Soames, and had become Stinker's best friend.

The Haven was also a haven for the intrepid troupe of monkeys, who had helped in the great Jolly Roger animal emancipation. Martha and Abbie came arond after school every day to teach them Irish dancing, and they were actually getting pretty good.

ROVER'S RETURN!

Sam Hannigan Found

Local girl and internet sensation Sam Hannigan, of Doggie Dinners fame, who mysteriously vanished on Tuesday night after an appearance on the popular TV show Bryan Hoolihan's Midweek Madness, has returned to Clobberstown – in the company of none other than the well-known entrepreneur and dog biscuit tycoon Roger 'Jolly Roger' Fitzmaurice. Fitzmaurice, 53, has announced plans to fund a range of animal shelters that will be managed and run by Sam Hannigan, the first of which will be Hannigan's Haven, due to open here in Clobberstown in the coming weeks.

Sam, who recently dressed up in a dog costume for four days to raise funds for the cause, was interviewed in her normal guise as a red-headed young girl. She says she is delighted by Mr Fitzmaurice's generosity and gave the following statement to our reporter: 'We are thrilled that Jolly Roger Dog Biscuits™ will be backing our new animal shelters. I know that Roger himself is especially overjoyed to be giving us so much money; he has even donated animals from his own private zoo. And on top of all that, he has pledged to help muck out the animals three times a week – haven't you, Roger?' Mr Fitzmaurice's smile could not be wider, despite the strange grinding noise that nearly drowned out the interview.

'I want to give a great big thanks to everybody who donated money to Dinners for Dogs,' continued Sam. 'All of you, along with good old Roger here, have allowed this animal shelter project to happen.'

'They're better dancers than the Clontipper Academy girls anyway,' said Martha.

'Yup! And they've better personal hygiene too,' added Abbie.

Bruno got involved in caring for the animals but also spent a lot of time in Daddy Mike's inventing sheds, now surrounded in the garden by newly made animal barns and shelters. After all the adventures with the Brain Swap 3000, he had decided to become an inventor himself.

Nanny Gigg was happy to make dinners for all of the animals, constantly surprising them with her hare-brained combinations of different foods and her strange choice of hats, and Ajay and Sam were more than happy to feed the animals three times a day – before school, at home time and before bedtime.

Ajay brought Tadhg the Tarantula and the rest of his creepy-crawly menagerie of insects, lizards and snakes around for regular visits, all travelling in boxes with little air holes in the back of his dad's taxi.

Sam sighed in contentment as she looked in the mirror and brushed her fuzzy red hair. She had always wanted animals but could never afford to have any (other than Rover the goldfish); now she had loads of animals, all happy, cared for and well fed, and she had loads of money to look after them with. She even owned Barker now, the lovely, furry hound whose body she had lived in for four full days.

Sam Hannigan smiled wide at her reflection. She was one lucky dog.

CHAPTER FIVE
OGG'S DUVET DAY

Conor woke the next morning to the sound of his alarm clock. When he sleepily opened his eyes, the first thing they focused on was an A4 refill pad page taped to the chair beside his bed. It read: 'NOT A DREAM!' His eyes sprung open. OGG!

He jumped out of bed and hastily pulled his trousers on over his pyjama bottoms. He ran down the stairs, two at a time, not worrying about the racket he was making as he knew his mum had already gone to work in the old people's home. She was always up and out a couple of hours before Conor, leaving him to fend for himself with breakfast and getting to school.

He opened the front door and looked around the side of the house. There was Ogg, sitting outside the kennel, scratching his matted, hairy head. He looked like he had just woken up too. Conor was glad that the thick creeper bush kept Ogg hidden from the view of anyone walking up Clobberstown Crescent.

Ogg looked up. 'Con! Nor!' he said and smiled a huge, toothy smile.

So it wasn't a fluke, thought Conor. He CAN speak. Well, kind of.

Ogg got to his feet, which were huge and just as hairy as his arms. Conor took him by the hand and led him into the house, after first checking that no passersby or nosy neighbours were looking.

Ogg was a bit reluctant to go through the door, but Conor tugged him through. He supposed Ogg probably found the dark, drafty kennel to be more cave-like than this nice, warm house.

'Right, Ogg,' said Conor. 'I have to go to school soon. You'll have to stay here until I figure out what to do with you.'

He led the caveman into the kitchen. Ogg was so tall he was practically hitting his head off the top of the door frames.

'Are you hungry?' Conor asked.

Ogg looked down at him impassively.

Conor pointed to his mouth and added, 'You know, hungry? Are you starvin' Marvin? Fancy a bit of brekkie?'

'Brekk. Eee,' said Ogg.

'That's the spirit!' cried Conor, amazed at how quickly Ogg was catching on to the language. Conor himself was almost three years old before he spoke his first word, and, being the quiet boy he is, he hadn't spoken that many since.

Conor looked through the kitchen presses. 'Okay, we have cornflakes, shredded wheat, Wheetie-Wheels?' He handed Ogg the packet of Wheetie-Wheels. Ogg shook it. He sniffed it. He stuck out his big tongue and licked it.

'No!' said Conor, remembering how Ogg had eaten the chocolate bars, wrappers included. 'You have to open the packet first!'

Ogg looked at Conor quizzically, then understanding seemed to dawn. He ripped the cardboard packet apart, and Wheetie-Wheels went flying all over the kitchen in a massive explosion of sugary toasted wheat.

Conor sighed. 'Never mind. Mum won't be back until tonight, so I'll clean it up later. How about we cook something?' He opened the fridge. 'We have sausages, rashers, fish fingers, a little bit of custard … Do you like eggs, Ogg?' He held up an egg to Ogg.

Ogg's face lit up. He held one finger up and put his other hand under the fur he was wearing and rummaged around. After a moment he took out of his furs the biggest egg Conor had ever seen – it was so enormous it made the egg Conor was holding look like a Tic Tac in comparison.

It was a greenish-blue colour and looked like it may have been laid by a prehistoric ostrich or emu. Ogg's hand, as colossal as it was, could barely hold it. 'Ogg. Egg. Ogg,' said Ogg.

Conor shook his head in wonder, shrugged his shoulders and took out the biggest frying pan he could find. Even that didn't seem big enough for Ogg's mega-egg, so Conor got up on a chair, climbed onto the kitchen worktop and reached up to take down the wok from the top of the press. His mum had bought it for cooking Chinese food, but she worked so much she never got time to cook any more.

Conor turned on the stove, heated some oil in the wok and, with Ogg's help, broke the heavy egg into it. The smell from the egg was ATROCIOUS! Conor had to take a kitchen chair and sit down! He pulled the neck of his school jumper over his face and opened up the window. He looked like a bandit from a cowboy movie, but at least it kept the stench out. Ogg looked delighted, standing over the wok as the egg cooked and licking his lips.

Conor wondered what a six-thousand-year-old egg would taste like and then decided he actually never wanted to find out.

When the egg was done, Conor had to use a garden spade to lift it out of the wok – none of the ordinary kitchen implements were big enough to shift it. He put it on a plate, and while he gathered up the huge bits of broken, jagged eggshell and put them in a bin bag, Ogg tucked in. He ate with no knife and fork, using only his bulky, sausage-like fingers. He smacked his lips as he ate, wiping his nose with his hairy forearm.

When he was finished, Ogg sat back happily in the chair and let out the loudest **BBuUuUuUuURRrRrRRPpPpPPP!** Conor had ever heard. He checked out the front window to make sure nobody else on the road had overheard Ogg's prodigious wind-breaking, but all out on Clobberstown Crescent – unlike in Conor's kitchen – was quiet.

Conor checked his watch. Time to go. 'Okay, Ogg,' he said, leading Ogg into the living room and sitting him down on the sofa, 'I have to go to school now. You will have to stay here until I get back.'

Ogg looked up at him from the sofa. 'BE GOOD,' said Conor. 'Don't answer the door. Don't answer the phone. Just sit here and watch the telly, and when I'm back I'll figure out what to do with you.'

Conor switched on the television, which came to life with colours and noises blaring. Ogg jumped up and hid behind the sofa. 'It's okay, it's okay,' said Conor. 'It's only morning TV, but I'm sure you'll find something you want to watch.'

He went into the kitchen and returned with the half empty, half torn apart packet of Wheetie-Wheels. 'Eat some of these if you get hungry again,' said Conor, and Ogg's head popped up slowly from behind the sofa. He could smell the Wheetie-Wheels.

As soon as Ogg was sitting back on the sofa with the Wheetie-Wheels packet in his lap, Conor grabbed his school bag and ran to the door. 'See you later, Ogg!' he whispered, not wanting the neighbours to hear. He closed the door quietly and set off for school, hoping that the six-thousand-year-old caveman he had left sitting on his couch wouldn't wreck his house.

Conor hadn't even reached his garden gate when his phone beeped. For one mad second he thought it was Ogg texting him, but he shook that crazy idea away – the caveman seemed to be very good at picking up words, but picking up a mobile phone and sending a text? Conor didn't think so.

He looked at his phone; it was from Charlie.

HOW IS R LITLE FREND? it read.

FINE, he texted back.

He was as economical with the written word as he was with the spoken word. Besides that, it is dangerous to text while you are walking down the street – you could be so distracted you could easily walk out under a bus.

Alan Nolan lives and works in Bray, County Wicklow, Ireland. He is co-creator (with Ian Whelan) of *Sancho* comic which was shortlisted for two Eagle awards, and is the author and illustrator of *The Big Break Detectives Casebook*, the 'Murder Can Be Fatal' series, *Fintan's Fifteen* and *Conor's Caveman* (The O'Brien Press).

Special thanks to my lovely editors Nicola Reddy and Aoife Walsh, and to Michael O'Brien, Emma Byrne, Ivan O'Brien and all at The O'Brien Press.

And extra-special thanks, as ever, to my long-suffering family, Rachel, Adam, Matthew and Sam.

www.SAMHANNIGANBOOK.com

www.ALANNOLAN.ie

www.OBRIEN.ie

From tots to teens and in between!

Visit **www.obrien.ie** for more brilliant books from
The O'Brien Press

Discover your next adventure today with our wide
range of children's books from great authors.

There's something for readers of all ages – historical fiction,
picture books, sport, graphic novels, young adult fiction
and lots more!

Read a sample chapter from one of our books or watch an
author video – and make sure to keep an eye out for special
offers and competitions.

Just for schools:

We have hundreds of resources for schools, including
teaching guides and activity sheets, all created by teachers for
teachers to make it so easy to bring our novels into your classroom.

All FREE to download today!